HOW TO SEX YOUR SNAKE

A JUNE NASH MYSTERY

MELISSA BANCZAK

Good Adventures!

[signature]

Good
Adventures

Cover Design - https://miblart.com
Compass Art - Jeremy Webb
Interior map - Laura Lynn Hardy
Editing by Lisa Mahoney - YourWriteWay@gmail.com
Contact the author at mel@melissabanczak.com

For James who shoulda had the first read

Smoochous to Mark

ACKNOWLEDGMENTS

Despite the year that I spent caring for my husband's 20 plus snakes (while he was stationed overseas during our military days) and that one time I rode in the back of a police car, I'm no expert on reptiles or crime. Many thanks to the ones who are and were such good sports about answering what probably felt like an endless stream of questions. Any factual errors are solely mine and not the fault of: Retired police officer, David *for the love of God make sure you never put evidence in a plastic bag* Vitkus, Herpetologist Sal *holy crap he owns a lot of creepy crawlies* Scibetta, and RN Angie *sure we can talk about bloody head wounds over Thanksgiving dinner* Dennison.

Thanks to my good friend Rosie *yeah I'll read it one more time* Zwaduk for reading the blasted book just one more time and to my husband Mark *don't you want to get up from your desk and go outside for a bit* Banczak. His patience and support always keep me going.

Lastly, this book would not have been possible without my extraordinary editor Lisa *doesn't mind when I stare at her blankly while she explains parts of speech* Mahoney. A writer is nothing without her editor.

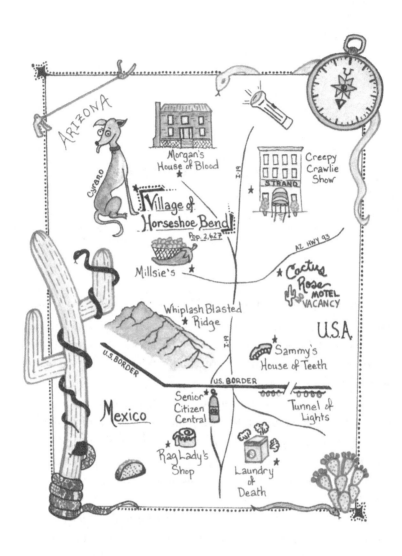

HOW TO SEX YOUR SNAKE

1

I was going too fast. Gravel was spinning out from under the wheels of my pickup and I could feel the tires slipping, threatening to launch me into the grove of prickly pear cactus that ran the length of the curvy road. Or was it cacti? *Blast.* I didn't care. I just wanted to get this over with. I tightened my grip on ten and two and pressed my slippered foot down on the gas.

When a mailbox appeared, I hung a hard left and steered up a rock-lined drive until it opened into a field. A rickety two-story farmhouse popped into view for a second before I spun the truck till I was facing the main road again and slammed on the brakes. My purse took a nose dive off the bench seat and spilled its guts all over the floorboards.

I really had to start zipping that thing. My wallet, cell phone and assorted bits of life were now buried ankle deep in the stuff that normally lived in the no man's land under the seat. I'd have to pick through it all later. For now, I wiggled the rearview mirror till I had a good view of the narrow steps leading up to the front door and laid on the horn. The sound scattered a flock of doves from a cluster of scrawny mesquite trees in the front yard and I instinctively ducked as they flew over the truck.

Somewhere, deep in the pile of stuff, my cell phone rang. I kicked my feet around and hit something solid. Instead of a phone, I found myself holding a pocket-sized volume titled, *20 Minutes to Death: 12 Fatal Black Mamba Encounters*, by Dewey Nash, *star of television's number one nature show, Gone Herpin'!* Ah, my prolific twin brother. He really knew how to grab his audience. In the three years since the show had made him an international TV star, he had written eight bestsellers.

As my cell continued to ring, I flipped the slim book over and looked down at the photo of Dewey. A pair of cloudy gray eyes peered out from under locks of shoulder-length, curly black hair, while the upturned collar of a brown leather jacket protected against an imagined breeze. Above the photo, a series of blurbs sang praise for the author. All were filled with words like thrill-seeker and daredevil and prominently featured some play on the words *sex appeal*.

While my brother and I aren't identical, it's easy to see that we're siblings. We've got the same hair. Though mine is usually contained in a thick ponytail. Same face. Same eyes. On my brother the image evokes an air of mystery and romance. On me? The urge for people to ask if I'm lost.

With a grunt, I tossed the book on the passenger floor and kicked my feet around till I found my phone. I managed to unlock the screen and answer before it stopped ringing.

"June, you need to come inside," Dewey said.

I really didn't need to do anything of the sort. This was Morgan's place and my no-Morgan streak was holding strong at nine years, eleven months and seven days. There was no way I was going to break that when I was so close to an even decade.

"I have office stuff to get back to," I said. And I did. As Dewey's personal assistant, I answer his fan mail, set up his appearance schedule and run interference from his hardcore fans, the *Dewzers*. And while it might not sound like much, it easily fills my days. Till this morning, we'd been in Costa Rica on a three-week shoot, and I hadn't been able to check my messages or log into my email because, as it just so happens, there's no Internet in the jungle. We'd landed at two in the afternoon. Dewey had mumbled something about...something. Maybe children with eating disorders. I hadn't really been listening. He'd taken our suitcases and disappeared into a waiting cab for home. Since I was never really off the clock and since there was a big twenty-city book tour coming up, I'd gone straight to my favorite dive for a greasy cheeseburger and a relatively stable WIFI connection. I'd only waded through a quarter of my messages when Dewey had texted, *meet me at Morgan's*. I'd ignored him. All I wanted to do was finish my work, so I could get home and jump in the hot tub. I desperately needed to soak a few layers of rain forest out of my pores. And of course, there was my no-Morgan streak to consider. Dewey's next text said my job was at stake, so here I was.

"You need to start leaving your Mustang at the airfield," I said.

When *Gone Herpin'* became the number one show on the Roar and Soar network, Dewey's agent had negotiated not only the use of a private jet, but also a salary ridiculous enough that Dewey could live anywhere he wanted. In the blink of an eye, my brother had us back in the sleepy little town where we'd grown up, nineteen dusty miles from the Mexican border, the Village of Horseshoe Bend, Arizona. Population 2,627. It wouldn't have been *my* first choice but he likes wandering the hills looking for reptiles and I like the money he pays me to be his assistant, so Horseshoe Bend it is.

"Just come inside."

"Why the drama?" I asked. "This isn't about me and Morgan, is it?"

In the three months that we'd been home, Dewey had been on a non-stop crusade to get me to bury the hatchet with his best friend.

"Just hurry up." He disconnected before I could say no.

"Blast." Dewey's popularity and my mouth made steering

clear of going viral a constant challenge. I'd been trying to cut back on my cursing since I'd come to work for my brother. You never knew when a tirade was going to end up on Youtube, autotuned by a creative fan.

I got out and slammed the truck door.

The doves, who'd settled on some feeders in the side yard, took off with an angry fluttering of wings. I caught a flash of red among the brown bodied birds and shielded my eyes for a better look. When the flock turned into the burning intensity of the desert sun, I flinched and looked away. It was probably somebody's lost macaw.

At the front porch I ignored the black metal railing that looked as unstable as the house, took the concrete steps in two strides and pounded a fist on the door. It wasn't latched and as it swung wide, I choked. The inside of Morgan's house smelled like an active sawmill.

"Dewey?" My eyes didn't want to adjust to the blackness of the front room. I leaned in the door to feel around for a light switch and came up empty. Blast. Who didn't have a light switch next to their front door? "Dewey, I'm here."

There was no answer.

If he thought I was hanging around all day… I stormed in, expecting to sink into a couple of inches of sawdust. Instead, I skidded over some sort of sticky mess, went head over heels and landed hard on my right hip and hand. A thin layer of goo squished under my various body parts as I pushed myself up off the bare wood floor. *Eww. What were the boys doing in here?*

"June?" Dewey sounded far away. And then pounding footsteps brought his voice closer. "Did you fall?"

"There's something sticky all over the floor." I wiped my fingers on my shirt and they bounced down the fabric.

"Don't move, you'll track it all over," Dewey called out. "Just give me a second. There's a switch in the hall here somewhere."

I flashed on the idea of Morgan coming home with a bag of groceries and dropping a gallon jug of syrup on the floor. He'd always been a bit of a klutz as a kid. *No.* His dog would have had fun with a mapley spill. Wait. *His dog.* Morgan had a dog. And while she sounded like the sweetest thing in the world, she was, from all accounts, the dumbest. Her longest running issue was remembering how a doggie door worked. After cleaning up the umpteenth puddle of piss, left on the floor directly in front of the escape hatch, Morgan finally gave up and started leaving the backyard sliding glass door open. All the time.

Since whatever I slipped in was too thick to be pee, I started thinking about the other thing that comes out of dogs. And just like the fool who touches a hot plate, I lifted my fingers to my nose and sniffed. Instead of the expected doggie by-product though, I inhaled the distinct aroma of hot pennies.

My mouth went dry and my stomach tried to crawl up my throat. I was the daughter of a nurse. If you weren't rolling change, the smell of copper meant only one thing.

"Found it," Dewey called out.

I blinked when the tiny entryway filled with light. And then I screamed.

I was standing in a drying pool of blood.

2

"**S**hut up, June."

Was I making that dreadful noise? I swallowed the rest of the scream and opened my eyes. An oversized metal claw snapped dangerously close to my nose. It was at one end of a three-foot pole. Dewey was at the other.

"You're okay." He snapped the snake tongs at me like that decided it.

Was I okay? I didn't think so. I was thinking I needed to scream some more.

Dewey read my mind and shook his head. "You'll be fine." He threw the tongs into the hall and then dug his cell phone out of a pocket. His right thumb danced over the keys as the other hand wagged a finger at me. "Don't look down."

Of course, I immediately did. Hey, where were my slippers? I turned and followed the reddish brown smears back to the door. There they were. Where I'd just been. In that sticky puddle. Of blood.

My feet kicked into action. I skidded and skipped and another scream, probably one of my own, chased me past a steep wooden staircase and down a cramped dark hall to the first door on the right. I reached for the knob as my shoulder hit the door. It flew open, hit the inside wall and bounced back into my face. My scream dissolved into a squeak and I dropped onto my butt.

Ow.

A shaft of soft light cut into the hall and I glanced up as the bathroom door drifted back open. Inside, I caught sight of the faded yellow shower curtain and for a hot second I was ten again and Morgan's mother was dead drunk, sprawled out in the tub, a spilled bottle of booze on the floor near the mat. She hadn't even raised her head when I'd flushed the toilet.

Tingling brought me back to reality. I lifted a hand to touch my sore nose and I caught sight of the red stuff on my fingers. Then I remembered why I'd headed this way in the first place and I scrambled to my feet.

I was torn between showering and puking. The former won out and I threw a foot over the edge of the tub, lost my balance and fell into the curtain.

The more I tried to get free, the more it seemed to fold itself around me. No. Wait. Someone was trying to wrap me up. Fists formed. I punched wildly connecting at least once before I was pushed against the wall of the shower with my arms pinned over my head.

"Hold still June, you're tangled in the curtain."

Warren?

The plastic peeled away from my face and I focused my eyes on the tin star above the breast pocket of the sheriff's uniform.

"Is Mom with you?"

When Dewey and I were little, and Sheriff Warren Mitchell was a fresh-faced deputy, he spent a lot of time at the clinic where our mom worked as a nurse. While our little town wasn't exactly filled to the brim with criminals, the ones we did have tended to take the saying *don't go down without a fight* to heart. And Warren was always happy to oblige. Mom patched him up so often that it didn't surprise anyone when she started bringing him home for coffee. Dewey and I weren't the swiftest of kids. It was quite a while before we realized what that meant. Twenty years later, Mom and Sheriff Mitchell were still having coffee a couple of times a week.

"It's just me." Warren sighed and rubbed at his eye with the back of his wrist. "You got me pretty good," he said. "How's your hand?"

I looked down. My knuckles on my right hand were bright red. "Should that hurt?" I asked.

"It will. You're in shock."

"What are you doing here?"

"Your brother had sense enough to text me."

"And you were nearby?" There was nothing near Morgan's house. Except Mom's. Her backyard was less than a football field away. Oh jeez. Dewey and I had interrupted a pot of coffee. I could feel my face flush and I dropped my eyes.

"You mother wasn't home. I was just leaving her a note...*hey*," Warren grabbed my arms and lifted them up. "Don't put your hands in your pockets."

"Why?" I looked down at my fingers. Oh yeah, I was covered in blood. My stomach gurgled and I launched myself at the toilet conveniently wedged between the shower and the sink.

"No!" Warren caught my shoulder, stopping my forward motion and snatched the hat off his head. He swung it under my mouth just as I gave up the burger I'd scarfed earlier at Millsie's. When my stomach was empty, I straightened up.

"Sorry," I said. "I was aiming for the toilet."

"I know," he said. "I can't have you contaminating my crime scene." He eyed the mangled shower curtain, now lying across the edge of the tub and added, "anymore." He stared at it for a bit and then let go of me to dig his cell phone from a pocket. While he studied the screen, I crouched down in the shower and shut my eyes. I felt loopy, like I'd had too many shots of Zacapa on an empty stomach.

"June? Are you okay? You're not going to faint, are you?" Warren's voice had a panicky edge to it and I almost smiled. It had been a while since he'd played the part of surrogate father. I hadn't realized how much I'd missed it.

"One of my guys needs to collect evidence. It's going to make things difficult if you faint in there."

So much for substitute dad. But I suppose the cop-flavored worries took precedence.

"You want to open your eyes?" he asked.

"You want me to puke again?" I had a good feeling I could go the distance.

"I've only got one hat," he muttered. "Keep 'em shut."

After a moment, I could hear shuffling around the room and then I was poked and prodded. And possibly bathed. I hummed to myself and tried to think about anything but blood. Of course, all I could think about was blood. Okay. New tactic. How did that song go? When you're freaked out and probably in shock, count all your favorite things? What *were* my favorite things? There weren't a lot. Dewey and I always seemed to be working. Though there *was* that time engine trouble stranded us in Cancun. I flashed back to the beachfront hotel. That was *one*. The heated pool with the swim-up bar. That was *two*. The smooth smoky rum poured into tall, tinted shot glasses. *Three*. The bartender who was getting off shift in fifteen minutes. *Four*. The hand-in-hand stroll toward that secluded spot through the coconut palms…

"June?"

"Five," I muttered.

"What?" Warren sounded concerned again.

Blast. Had I said my list out loud?

"June. Can you take off your clothes?"

My eyes popped open. That had been the next thing on my list but it certainly wasn't something I wanted to hear my mom's friend-with-benefits say to me.

Warren cleared his throat and looked away. "We need your clothes."

I glanced over at the deputy crouched down in front of what could have been a giant tackle box and shook my head. "So do I."

"You can put these on," Warren said.

I squinted at the neon orange fabric in his hands. "I don't think so. What's going on Warren?" I swallowed and bobbed my head in the general direction of that sticky puddle of blood. "Where's Dewey? Is he okay?"

He ignored me and shouted at the hall, "Is Stober here yet?"

"Warren?"

He gave me a healthy dose of cop face and I shut up. There was no point in trying to talk to him when he was like this.

A woman about my age stepped into the room. Her tall athletic body was decked out in a black leather ensemble that got a sideways glance of approval from the deputy: over-the-knee boots, mini skirt, vest, and long, blond hair woven into a braid that hung down the back of her waist-high jacket. The only things about her that screamed crime scene were the purple booties and gloves. And maybe the huge duffel bag she was carrying that had the Horseshoe Bend Sheriff's department logo embroidered on the side.

I must have been staring. She smoothed an imaginary wrinkle in her skirt and muttered, "I was off duty."

Warren cleared his throat. "Stober will collect your things." Then he wagged a finger in my face. "Do not take forever. Do not get back in the tub." *Hey, how'd I get out of the tub?* "And above all, do not touch anything else." He laid the neon stuff on the strip of butcher paper that was now covering the bathmat and disappeared out the door. The deputy lingered just a moment.

"You should talk to your doctor about your exposure to unknown blood. Preferably today."

Great. Not only was I possibly contaminated in some death-inducing way, but if I checked in with my own doctor, Mom was sure to find out, determine this was all my fault and then lecture me till I died from whatever I'd been exposed to. My only hope was the clinic on 27th street. Mom and the lady who ran it weren't currently on speaking terms. Something about...something. Maybe soccer? I hadn't been paying attention to the rant when I drove Mom home from the bar fight. And just in case the two had made up, a reasonable cash donation to the clinic would help keep the gossip from Mom's ears.

I realized the woman in leather was still standing there staring at me. I'd already forgotten her name so I just gave her an uncomfortable head bob. Was she going to stay?

"I have to confirm the chain of custody for your clothes," Leather Girl explained.

So that was a yes.

I never considered myself a prude but I guess I am because I did a half turn before I started stripping, handing stuff back over my shoulder as I went. My jeans, a low-cut, tight, v-neck t-shirt that worked best when I was bra-less, a brand new blueberry-colored thong, and my favorite hoodie were all probably ruined. On the other hand, skin that had been covered with clothing appeared to be blood free. So a win for me, I guess.

The neon stuff that Warren had left turned out to be running pants and a short-sleeved t-shirt that promoted a Halloween themed 5K. The fit was adequate but the hue was so bright that I could make out my reflection in the shower tile.

I heard Leather Girl's duffel bag zip. When I turned around she'd been replaced by Warren.

"Foot," he said.

"What?"

Warren reached down and lifted my leg by the ankle. He pulled something purple from his pocket and slipped it over my bare foot. "Other leg," he said and tapped a hand against the calf. A little hop and my other foot was buried in purple too. "Put these on," he said and my hands disappeared into matching gloves.

"Walk." He steered me out into the hall and pushed.

Somebody had turned on all the lights. I glanced over my shoulders looking for Dewey and caught sight of the trail of bloody footprints that led back to the front room. *My* bloody footprints. Blast. How did I get in the middle of whatever this was? And where was Dewey?

"Where's my brother?"

Warren ignored the question. "Walk." And then he twisted me away from the blood.

The booties were made to cover shoes so I had to scrunch my toes to keep them on. As I stumbled along, something nagged at the back of my brain. What was I forgetting? As we passed an open door, I dug in my heels and Warren almost tripped over me.

I let out a low whistle and stared into what could only be described as a hoarder's paradise. Snakes wiggled in dozens of cages that lined all four walls, floor to ceiling. In the center of the room, a table was covered in the same stuff that was always laying around Dewey's house: hooks on long handles, small pieces of gnarly twisted wood, empty water bowls in various sizes, and red light bulbs still in their protective packaging. A few bags of aspen shavings were stacked near the door. Dewey used that to line the cages for his creepy crawlies too. But his collection was nothing like this. Which explained why the house smelled like a sawmill. And why my brother had spent so much time here since we'd come back to town.

And then I remembered what I'd forgotten. *Morgan*. Where was he? After I'd fallen in the blood, and Dewey had come running from the back of the house, he'd been alone.

"Where's Morgan?" I wasn't sure I wanted an answer.

And from the look on Warren's face, I knew I wasn't getting one. He tightened his grip on my arm. "Come on."

We passed two more critter stuffed rooms before Warren stopped us outside a bedroom that looked like it would have fit into any normal house. "Did you open that slider?"

I peered in the cage-free room. Hey, was that Dewey's suit-case sitting next to the open slider? I leaned around the edge of the door for a better look. And there was mine on the floor of the master bath. The idiot had come here straight from the airport. Blast. Practically everything I owned was in that suitcase.

"That's mine," I said pointing, "do you think I could just...."

His look told me no.

Blast.

"June?"

"What?" *Oh yeah.* "No, I didn't open that slider."

Warren nodded and we continued on our way. At the end of the hall, he opened the side door, lifted up a strip of yellow crime scene tape and gave me a gentle shove. I stepped out onto the tiny porch and sighed. The sun was about to set and I was stuck in short sleeves. I gave my arms a preemptive rub.

"Are you cold?" Warren asked. "Have you got a sweater in your truck?"

I knew there was one in my suitcase. "Maybe." There *was* a lot of stuff in my truck.

"Go have a look." He gave me another gentle push and I was halfway down the stairs before I remembered why I was about to be freezing in the first place.

"No, wait. What's going on?"

"That's a good question, isn't it?" Warren asked. "I was having a nice quiet afternoon and the next thing I know I'm finding you and your brother at the scene of a possible crime. There's at least three liters of blood on that floor. You have any idea how it got there?"

"No. Ask Morgan."

"I'd love to." Warren dug a little notebook from a pocket, freed a short green pencil from the spiral binding and flipped to an empty page. "You have any idea where he might be?"

"He's not here?" I flashed on the sticky red puddle.

"When was the last time you saw him?"

Three liters of blood. How does somebody walk away from that?

"June?"

I shook away the image that was trying to form in my brain.

"When was the last time you saw Morgan?"

"I don't know. Graduation."

"From college?" Warren asked.

"From high school," I said.

Warren looked surprised. "You haven't seen Morgan once in the ten years since high school? You three were inseparable as kids."

Only out of necessity. Dewey liked hunting for snakes, Morgan had a car and I tagged along because it took me away from Mom's constant need to lecture me about pretty much everything I was doing wrong with my life. It had been a great arrangement.

Till Morgan decided to be a jerk. The image of a broken, bloody body tried to creep back into my brain. I shook it away.

"You and Dewey have been back almost three months. This is a small town. How could you not have seen Morgan?"

"Luck?"

Warren frowned at me and I shrugged.

"I don't know. I just haven't." I looked around for something else to focus on. The wooden fence that hid the backyard. Doves at the feeders. The path to my mom's house that cut through the field covered in prickly pear cactus. Cacti. *Cactus?*

"June?"

"Yeah?" I turned back to Warren.

"I thought Morgan was helping out on Dewey's show?"

"He is. He's doing PA work on local shoots."

The pencil paused over the paper. "PA?"

"Production Assistant. He helps out with whatever the guys on the shoot need help with. Carrying stuff, running errands...." *Bleeding to death, alone and afraid.* Blast. I hated Morgan. I really did.

"If he's Dewey's PA, why haven't you seen him at work?"

"I don't go on the local shoots."

"Okay." He started writing again. "You know anyone who had a beef with him?"

"No." Suddenly, my issues with the idiot didn't seem all that important.

"How about anyone *he* might have had a beef with?"

"Wait," I almost missed the emphasis. "Do you think that might be somebody else's blood?"

"One last question. What time did your plane land today?"

"I don't know." I'd had a watch when we'd left for Costa Rica. I forgot to zip my tent on day three and some sort of monkey snatched it. Along with the only bra I'd packed. "I didn't check. I just went straight to Millsies."

"I'll need to verify that with Alvaro." He stowed the pencil in the notebook's spiral binding and both disappeared back into his pocket. "Do you need a ride?"

"Do you really think that's Morgan's blood in there?"

All I got was cop face. "Do you need a ride?" he repeated.

I folded my arms. "I'll wait for Dewey."

"I think he's going to come down to the station with me."

"You're arresting him?" This was not good. Dewey didn't like being cooped up. It's why he was always wandering the hills. The critters he found were just a bonus. And then I had a truly horrifying thought. An arrest meant publicity and most networks didn't like it when their talent appeared on the news wearing handcuffs. Even when they later turned out to be innocent. If Dewey lost his best friend *and* his show....

"Did I say anything about arresting anyone?" Warren actually looked insulted. "I'm still trying to figure out what happened here. If you want to put a label on it, let's call your brother a person of interest."

"Dewey would never hurt anyone, especially Morgan. They're best friends." Despite *my* best efforts.

"That doesn't mean a lot in my line of work," Warren said.

"I'll be in touch if I have more questions. For now, you can go." He disappeared through the door and I heard the lock click behind him. I peeled off the gloves and hung them over the railing.

Warren was crazy if he thought he was getting rid of me that easily.

3

Warren's patrol car was in the driveway next to my pickup along with two other cars I didn't recognize. Someone had strung more of the yellow *Crime Scene Do Not Cross* tape around the edges of the yard. Not that there was a crowd threatening to cross. After mom's, the nearest house was probably three or four miles away. It was another reason we'd all spent so much time together as kids. You make do with what you got.

Morgan's front door was propped open and Leather Girl was on the steps, leaning into the house, talking to someone inside. She'd thrown a wind breaker over her outfit. One hand clutched the wrought iron railing while the other tugged at her skirt which was creeping up in back and threatening to give me a view I wasn't interested in seeing. Though, it *would* make us a tad even.

I tiptoed around to the back of my truck, silently cursing both the thin vinyl booties covering my feet and the chunks of gravel beneath them and peeked into the cargo bed. Maybe Dewey or I had thrown some footwear back there at some point in the past. Aside from a spare tire and some jumper cables, it was empty.

Blast.

"June." Dewey's voice was muffled, as if he was underwater. Or one car over in the backseat of Warren's cruiser. I step hopped around to the front, throwing a few of my favorite words down at the sharper stones chewing up the stupid purple booties and ripped open the driver's door.

"What's going on, Dewey?"

"I don't know. I swear. I didn't see the blood until you fell in it."

"Warren just asked me if I knew where Morgan was."

"He asked me too."

"And do you?"

"I don't have a clue."

"Did Morgan say where he was going?"

"Well…"

"Did he just leave suddenly?"

"Actually, I'm not sure he was ever home."

"What?" My voice echoed and I could see Leather Girl straighten and look out into the yard. I ducked down and waited till she turned back before I dropped onto the seat and slowly pulled the door till it clicked shut. "Okay. So when you got here, the blood wasn't there."

"I don't know, I went in Cyrano's door."

"Who?"

"Cyrano. Morgan's dog. I told you he leaves a door open cause she's got issues with the doggie door."

Oh yeah. The open slider in the bedroom.

"Was the dog inside?"

"I don't know."

"Come here," I motioned to Dewey. He leaned toward me and I flicked him on the forehead.

"Ow."

"Why did you go in the house if Morgan wasn't there?"

He rubbed his forehead with a palm. "He's got a bunch of new clutches. I wanted to see the triaspis."

I had no earthly idea what that meant so I did what I always do when I don't know what he's talking about. I offered a grunt and a quick nod.

As always, he wasn't fooled. "Senticolis triaspis," he hissed at me. "It's the scientific name for a Green Rat Snake. Jeez, June, you helped me photograph some for a chapter..." he paused to stare off into space and count on his fingers, "three...no four books ago." Then he let out a deep sigh. "I write bestsellers. Aren't you ever going to read any of them?"

I really had no desire. After spending the whole day listening to people talk about creepy crawlies, the last thing I wanted to do when I got home was read about them. I wasn't about to admit that to him though, so I changed the subject.

"You come here straight from the airport?" I asked.

"Yeah."

"That was like three hours ago. No wonder Warren's calling you a person of interest. How could you spend so much time in that house and not see the blood?"

"I was in with the snakes."

"All this time? What were you doing in there?"

He shrugged. "A few snakes pooped in their water...." *Eww.* "So after that I started checking all the dishes. I figure, I'm here, I got time, I may as well clean a few cages and wow, there's some excellent new specimens in his collection. Did you know that Morgan has a female juvenile Oxybelis aeneus? I've been dying to get us out to the Ridge since we moved back but we just haven't had time."

Whiplash Ridge. That sent a shiver down my spine. The place was a barren death trap. Steep hills, curvy roads, and a vast empty desert as far as they eye could see.

"*Morgan.* When did you talk to him last?" I laid my left hand on the passenger seat's headrest and Dewey eyed my fingers.

"I got a couple of texts. He wanted me to stop by because he was having trouble getting a baby from one of the new clutches to eat."

"Did he sound upset?" I asked.

"Yeah, it was one of the triaspis," he said.

"No, I mean did he sound like he was afraid someone was going to…." I flashed on all that blood and stopped myself before I added the words, *whack off his head*? I shook away an image that was forming. I needed to keep Morgan out of my thoughts. If I didn't, I was going to lose it. And right now, Dewey needed me. "If you didn't know about the blood, why did you make me come inside?" I asked.

"I wanted you to see all the baby snakes."

"Why?"

"Because they're cute. I thought maybe if you played with them you'd be more interested in what I do." He leaned back in the seat and shrugged his shoulders. "You don't like the job. You never have."

"That's not true," I said. Though it was. I hung around because it was Dewey. And he paid me a lot of money. And because it was Dewey.

"You hate all the mail I get, you hate going on location, you hate the Dewzers," he said.

"I don't hate…" I wasn't sure which option to go with. I hated all of it but I didn't trust anyone else to put my brother's interests first. "Listen. I love you. As long as you want me around, I'm not going anywhere."

I opened the car door.

"Where are you going?" he asked.

"To find Warren. Maybe he'll let me drive you to the station. I can't risk anyone seeing you in the back of a patrol car." I swung my left leg out onto the gravel driveway and caught sight of my purple clad tootsies. If I was going to be hoofing it around Morgan's gravel-covered yard, I needed a lot more than crime scene vinyl protecting my feet. "Give me your shoes and socks."

Dewey's boots were a couple of sizes too big so I stuffed the crime scene booties in the toes and tied the laces extra tight. As I got out, I wagged a finger at him. "Slouch down back there just in case somebody drives by and gets curious."

Over at the front door, Leather Girl was still distracted by whatever was happening inside the house and never heard me climb the porch steps. At the top, I leaned around her trying to look for Warren. I didn't see him but I did spot my high school chemistry teacher, Mr. Falito, headed my way. The name badge on his pocket had a big *CS* on it so I guessed he'd either moved onto a new career or was moonlighting. We made brief eye contact and then he quickly looked down. Blast. Did he think Dewey had something to do with all that blood too? As Mr. Falito stepped into the doorway and maneuvered around Leather Girl, he lifted his arm and I got a close-up view of the notes on the paper bag he was holding. The name Dewey Nash was neatly written on the line marked suspect. "What the hell?" I grabbed his arm for a better view.

Leather Girl, who'd been unaware of me, spun around and bumped into my former teacher who teetered on the lip of the top step before he lost his balance. I was left literally holding the bag as his arms swung wild, hands desperately grabbing at the air. He ended up with her wind breaker clutched in a fist and I could hear fabric rip as the two of them took out the porch railing and fell to the ground below in a tangled mess.

"June." Warren filled the open door.

"Dewey's a suspect now?"

He didn't answer. Instead, he took the evidence bag from me and dropped it into a box just inside the door. Then he gripped my shoulders, helped me down the stairs and twisted me in the direction of my truck. As I glanced back, Mr. Falito was making the mistake of trying to help Leather Girl adjust the skirt that had settled up around her waist, exposing her tiny yellow thong. Okay, *now* we were a tad closer to even.

"June, I'd like you to leave my crime scene now," Warren said.

I looked over at the cruiser. Dewey had his face twisted up against the back window, trying to keep us in sight and I thought about the reviews on the back of his last book. My daredevil brother looked more like a scared little kid and I needed to do something to help him. Trouble was, I had no idea what that something might be. I decided to stick with my best trait. Anger.

"What the hell, Warren. Five minutes ago Dewey was a person of interest. What changed?"

He planted his hands on his hips and gave me more of his cop attitude. "I'm not going to discuss my crime scene with you. My relationship with your mother does not give you special consideration."

"Relationship?" That was the first time I'd ever heard either of them refer to their coffee sessions as a relationship.

Warren wagged a finger at me. "Now don't go reading more into that than there is. If you want to do something to help, you can get in touch with your mom's friend Harrison Kim. Let him know what's going on."

"Dewey needs a lawyer?" Blast. That should have been my first thought.

"It's in his best interest." He spun me around and pushed me in the direction of my truck. I glanced back and he made a motion to keep going. Since it looked like there was nothing else I could do, I raised a hand toward the patrol car. Dewey returned the wave.

Over at my truck, I discovered that my keys were still in the ignition. I cranked the engine, gripped the steering wheel and yelped in pain. My knuckles were finally starting to hurt. I blew on them a couple of times and shifted into gear. As the truck roll forward, I could see Warren in the rearview mirror. He had his cell phone pressed to his chest and was waving at me. I slammed on the brakes and rolled down the window as he jogged over.

"I need you to go pick up your mom."

That was not something I wanted to do. "How about you take *me* to jail and Dewey goes and gets her?"

"June."

"She has her own car."

"Your mother is about to find out that her child is a person of interest in a possible murder investigation," Warren said. "She shouldn't be driving at a time like this."

"And *I* should? I'm the one who was rolling around in a pool of blood."

"You want to tell her that?" Warren asked.

Heck no.

He waved a dismissive hand at my truck and put the phone back to his ear. "Wendy, hang on, there's something I need to tell you."

As I watched him walk away, I hoped he realized that if he arrested Dewey, he'd be having coffee by himself for a very long time.

4

Mom was waiting outside the ER, tapping away on her phone, when I pulled into the parking lot. Her hair was making an escape from its scrunchy and she was still in her scrubs. Thanks to a chunk of Greek that was grafted onto the family tree via our misplaced dad, Dewey and I looked nothing like our pasty white, freckle-painted, red-headed mother.

I wasn't looking forward to the conversation we were about to have and half considered driving past. Of course, she chose that moment to look up. She grabbed a backpack from the curb and when she decided I'd slowed down enough, she ripped open the passenger door and hopped in.

"I don't understand what's going on, June. I thought everyone was still in Costa Rica." She kicked at the trash around her feet to make a space for her backpack.

"Hello to you too, Mom," I said, as I eased the car through the lot and back out onto the main road.

"I'm sorry, June. Are you experiencing something in your life that makes you more important than your incarcerated brother?"

Or his dead best friend. *Don't think about Morgan.*

"June, are you listening to me?" She twisted the rear-view

mirror her way, dug wipes out of the backpack and began to scrub a day in the ER off her face.

I cleared my head with one good shake.

"Dewey hasn't been arrested, Mom." I was hoping that was still true.

"Not yet," she said. She ripped the rest of her hair out of the scrunchy and began to work a brush through it.

The light ahead turned yellow and I eased my foot off the gas. The last thing I needed was one of mom's colorful anecdotes about safety.

"How could you let this happen? You're supposed to be looking out for your younger brother."

Ninety seconds and the stroke of midnight made me my brother's keeper.

"You're supposed to be the one with common sense," she added.

I put the truck in park and turned in my seat to look at her. "Why do I have to be the one with *oh Mom*." It wasn't a view of her face that I was treated to as she yanked off her scrub top. She tossed it on the floor then wiggled out of her pants. I never thought I'd be so happy to discover that my Mom wore granny panties. A granny bra would have been nice too. The guy in the car next to us honked his horn in appreciation, and a couple of people on the sidewalk stepped off the curb for a better look. She ignored them all.

"Mom, people can see you." I flipped down my sun visor. At least I didn't have to watch them watching us.

"I like to look nice in public," she said. I could feel her eyes giving my neon outfit a once over. Thankfully, she didn't ask. Instead, she fished a skirt and blouse out of the backpack then jerked a thumb at the windshield. "Green light."

"Mom, would you just get dressed," I said.

"Oh honestly, June. You're such a prude."

I was tempted to tell her that I'd recently stripped for another woman but I didn't. Too many unanswerable questions would follow.

As we moved through the intersection a flash of red on a telephone wire caught my eye. Was that the same bird from Morgan's yard? I leaned against the wheel and craned my neck for a better look. It was certainly the same size as the other bird.

"June," Mom shrieked.

I looked down in time to swerve back into our lane and avoid the Volkswagen and its finger-waving horn-honking driver coming at us. When I glanced back up, the bird was gone. For the rest of the ride I was treated to a painstakingly detailed anecdote involving a motorcycle, a pit of gravel and a shirtless idiot. I didn't see how a little lane drifting had anything to do with being an idiot on purpose, but I held my tongue.

The sun had set by the time we pulled up to the sheriff's station. The main drag, Rouse Boulevard, was empty. I didn't see any patrol cars, which meant that Warren had brought Dewey in through the back alley. That would keep the media off our backs. For a while anyway.

Mom was out of the truck before I could put it in park. I hung back. I didn't want to be around in case anyone mentioned finding me covered in blood. *Don't think about Morgan.* I'd had enough lectures for one night. And I needed to grab my jacket. I rubbed the goosebumps on my bare arms and jogged across the deserted street.

Downtown Horseshoe Bend is populated with the same three blocks you see in every small town. A couple of banks, the post office, the hardware store, a bakery, old-lady consignment shops, a decrepit professional building with a faded *space available* sign and half a dozen hole-in-the-wall eateries-slash-bars. My office was on the third floor of a building that housed my favorite: Millsie's.

I went in the front and cut through the empty bar. Everyone who rented space in the building was supposed to use the street entrance to their offices. But the stairs to the third floor were dark and steep, and Millsie's had a service elevator left over from the building's days as a swanky hotel. So I cheated. As long as I usually ordered something on my way through, no one seemed to care.

Alvaro, Millsie's owner, was on a stool at the counter video chatting with his granddaughter.

"The Chief called looking for you earlier." He squinted at my outfit but kept any thoughts about it to himself.

"He found me," I said.

"Say hello to Ingrid." He turned his laptop in my direction. "She's coming down to visit this weekend." The girl lived in Tucson and came down almost every weekend. Alvaro always treated it like it was a rare occasion.

I waved at the thirteen-year-old on the screen, careful not to slow my stride. She was decked out in a homemade *Dewzer Girl* t-shirt and had some sort of snake draped around her neck. Half of its body was woven through her thick brown hair and around one of the arms of her glasses. Part of me wanted to shriek in terror. Not because of the snake. But because of the shirt.

Dewzers, the rabid fans of Dewey's show, Gone Herpin', often feel a need to share with me, in excruciating detail, the things they'd enjoy doing to him, always forgetting that their object of desire is my baby brother. By ninety seconds and the stroke of midnight. To bypass the therapist chair, I avoid anyone who might be a *Dewzer*. I have no social media accounts, I ignore random people on the street, and I merely skim the hundreds of letters he gets each week. If it's from a sick child, I arrange a one-on-one. If it's a horny adult, and they include a self-addressed stamped envelope, they get a glossy 8x10 onto which I inscribe with a silver sharpie, *Good Adventures, Dewey Nash*. That's the catch phrase he uses to end every episode of his show. If there's no SASE, then into the trash the envelope goes.

"Is Dewey with you? Did he get my letter?"

At thirteen, she kinda fell into the adult category and I couldn't remember when she'd written last or if she'd included a

SASE. Besides, the girl had about a dozen autographed photos already. "He had to..." nothing came to mind so I finished with, "I really need to..." and I was through to the kitchen. As the two-way door swung shut, I could hear her last words chase after me.

"Tell him my new email is Ingrid-the-snake-charmer at gmail dot com. Good Adventures."

Yeah right. Like I'd ever give my brother a teenage girl's email address.

I waved a hand at the night cook, Garrett. "Nothing for now." As the door to the service elevator slid shut, I watched one of his fingers disappear up a nostril. Okay, nothing later either.

On the third floor, I took a left and went down two spots to my office. Chances were pretty good that I had a hoodie thrown over the back of a chair for shivering emergencies, which happen in the desert more often than you'd think. I had enough time to grab it and run over to the 27th Street Clinic for some quick *am I going to die from exposure to all that blood* testing and then get back to the sheriff's station before mom noticed that I was gone. I was counting on her being preoccupied with Dewey and Warren for a while. Considering that her boyfriend was holding her son as a person of interest in a possible murder case, I probably had a lot of time to kill.

I turned my key in the lock and stepped inside. And gagged. The air was stale and the place smelled like a locker room thanks to me leaving the air conditioner off. I flipped on a light. Or maybe my office smelled that way because someone really messy was living in it.

Clothes spilled out of a gym bag by the door and a layer of red dirt led across the parquet floor to the little sitting area. My glass coffee table had been moved against the wall and the futon was open and covered in a tangled mix of blankets and sheets. More remnants of dirty shoes led into the half bath on my left where takeout bags overwhelmed the tiny trashcan. Back at my desk, a pair of jeans was slung over the armrest of my high back chair and above that a long sleeved green gingham and a t-shirt featuring the stacked silhouette of a curvy woman were tacked to my bulletin board. I touched one of the gingham's sleeves and it had that stiff air dry feel to it. Laundry?

Okay this was weird.

I stood in the middle of the room, not sure what to do. Whoever was squatting wasn't around at the moment. Was it safe to be here? Would they return? And how did they get in my office in the first place? I went back to the door and checked the lock. It hadn't been jimmied so how did they get in? Only a few people had keys. Me...Dewey...Mom...*Morgan.*

I had a vague recollection of Dewey telling me that he was giving a key to Morgan so he could do something or other. From the looks of things, it had been to move in.

I went to my desk. A wrinkled map of the United States was spread out over the top. Someone had made illegible notes all over it in handwriting that looked pretty similar to the scrawl on Morgan's Christmas cards. If he'd really been here, I needed to call Warren. I found the phone underneath. As I lifted the receiver, I leaned against my chair and casually ran a thumb over the jeans. They felt clean. And soft. Really soft. And they weren't neon orange. I dropped the receiver back in the cradle and held them up against my hips. They were long but if I cuffed them.... I set them back down. No. Morgan was slim but he was a good three inches taller than me and he was a guy. There was no way they'd fit. Besides, Warren'd be pissed if he knew I'd messed with what he'd probably consider another crime scene. I dropped the jeans and snatched up the telephone receiver. And then set it back down. Still....

When had he been here? I went to the trash and took a look at the bag on top. A take-out receipt stapled to the side was dated almost a week ago. The blood in Morgan's house was maybe a day old. Chances were good that Morgan camping out in my office had nothing to do with whatever happened at his house. I didn't really believe that but at this point I didn't care. I ran my thumb down the jeans again. They were really soft.

~

After a quick stop at the ATM and a few pokes, prods, and promises to return to the 27th Street Clinic for followups, I was back at the sheriff's station standing before Moira's reception desk. Mom was nowhere in sight. I wasn't sure what to do next. Warren hadn't been specific beyond, get mom, meet him at the station.

I sighed and jammed my hands into the jean pockets. They went in well past my wrists. Hey, how come women's jeans didn't have pockets like these? I rocked back on my heels and hiked the waist up a bit. Even without a belt, they fit better than I would have liked anyone to know. I'd thrown the long sleeved gingham on over the t-shirt and buttoned up till most of the curvy silhouette was covered. Last thing I needed from mom was a lecture about my appearance. I'd certainly skirted by earlier. While I waited for Moira to notice me, I glanced around. The compact squad room behind her, usually manned by a couple of deputies, was empty and the place was deathly quiet except for the sound of Moira's fingernails tapping away at her computer keyboard. I sighed again. I needed a distraction soon or I was going to start thinking about things I didn't want to think about.

"Did anybody bring some suitcases back from Morgan's place?"

"I have no idea," she said without looking up. "I don't log evidence."

"Cause everything I own is in my suitcase. And Dewey had it at Morgan's." I couldn't wear Morgan's jeans forever. He'd want them back at some point. Assuming he was still in one piece. *All that blood.* Blast. I felt lightheaded and grabbed the edge of the counter.

"You all right?" Moira was watching me with an alarmed look on her face.

"Yeah." *Don't think about the blood.*

"The Chief's not back yet. Your mom's in his office." She grinned at me. "You want to go back and wait with her?" Oh, she knew me so well.

I jerked a thumb at the empty room behind her. "Where's everybody else?"

"It's Metal Fest this weekend."

That explained the empty streets. And Leather Girl's attire.

"You need something to do?" Moira extended a hand. A sticky note dangled from her index finger. I tilted my head to read it. *Cactus Rose. Room 11. Snake.*

The Cactus Rose motel was out on old state highway 93, about twenty miles outside of town. It had been popular back in the days when families took road trips. Today, it was more conducive to those who enjoyed their afternoon quickies in a spot off the beaten path.

I needed a distraction but creepy crawlies didn't count. "No thanks. Snakes are Dewey's thing."

Moira leaned back in her seat and raised her eyebrows.

At least they were when he wasn't a person of interest. "Well, who'd you call before we moved back?" I asked.

"Morgan."

I guess she'd been briefed about what was going on.

She waved a hand around the room. "At the moment, I've got no one else and the lady on the phone was pretty insistent I send someone right away."

Blast.

"What about H.A.H.?" I asked.

The Herpetology Association of Horseshoe Bend wasn't really an association. It was more like a dozen reptile geeks that cruised the back roads on weekends looking for snakes.

Moira shook her head. "Chief would kill me if I called them in an official capacity."

He probably would. Warren and his deputies consider H.A.H. a menace. They drive slow, stop on a dime and abruptly leap out of cars to huddle around what often turns out to be a stick in the middle of the road.

"You hang out with them though, right?" she asked.

Dewey and Morgan did. I'd tagged along once when we were in high school. After what felt like the hundredth break slam of the night, I'd puked all over three of the H.A.H. members and was dis-invited to all future outings for the rest of my natural life. The guy who'd ended up with most of the chunkiest stuff in his lap had been very specific.

I considered the yellow sticky note on the end of Moira's finger and sighed. Even if I wanted to ask H.A.H. for help, I probably wasn't going to be able to get a hold of any of them. Chances were really good that they were out cruising Whiplash Ridge. Phone service on the Ridge was non existent. And even if by some miracle I *was* able to reach one of them, sooner or later, they were going to ask about Dewey. Or Morgan.

Morgan.

"Fine." I snatched the note off her finger. And after a lifetime of watching Dewey *rescue snakes from silly people*, as he like to put it, I was pretty sure I could handle a solo run. And I did need the distraction.

"They speak English?"

Since a third of Horseshoe Bend's population had been in the area since Mexico had owned what was now Arizona, it was always a toss-up.

"She sounded adequately proficient."

Perfect. Since my grasp of Spanish wasn't.

"Let 'em know I'm on my way."

Moira rocked back in her chair and raised her eyebrows at me. "Good Adventures."

I growled at her and then headed back across Rouse Boulevard as a crappy little Honda pulled up outside Millsie's front door. The driver, a scruffy looking guy with wild hair and a crazy beard, waved like he knew me. Last thing I needed was some off-beat acquaintance asking about Dewey. Before the guy could get out of his car, I dove into the dark, creepy, street entrance to the third floor and locked the door behind me. In case he decided to hang around, I'd sneak out through the alley and take the long way back to my car.

Upstairs, just inside my office door, I grabbed an orange bucket knowing that Dewey kept it filled with everything I'd need. From the back of a closet, I dug out the pair of snake tongs that I'd ordered for him for our birthday. I had no idea what was waiting for me at the motel and the triple coated rubber top jaw made them ideal for handling combative species. And Dewey said I never listened to him.

5

I slid my truck into a spot by the motel office and let the engine idle. The Cactus Rose Motel is your typical old-style motor lodge with a single strip of cheap rooms and a square concrete pool at the far end of the parking lot. Overhead, a giant neon-green cactus with a vacancy sign fizzled on and off and cast everything in an eerie glow. At the end of the strip near the pool I could just make out a housekeeping cart, jammed in a half-open door at an angle. That was probably room eleven. I shut off the truck and grabbed the bucket and tongs. The motel office was empty so I headed for the cart.

There were two lone cars in the parking lot, and as I passed the second one, I heard a lock click and a figure popped out. She was a little thing. Maybe five feet and lost in a dark blue maid's uniform that doubled as an ugly mu-mu. Her yellow gloved hands clutched a spray bottle as if it offered some sort of protection against the world outside of her locked car.

"Are you here for the snake?" she asked eying the tongs.

I wondered how often people checked-in with props.

"Yeah. How big is it?" Size would determine just how much of an effort I put into finding the thing.

The maid pursed her lips and shivered a bit. "Big."

Okay, so one quick pass then.

When we reached room eleven, I set down the bucket and leaned the tongs against the wall. The cart was wedged in there pretty good. What would Dewey do first? Probably make sure he didn't run the snake over trying to clear the doorway. I pulled on a pair of leather gloves from the bucket and dropped to one knee.

There was nothing around the wheels except scattered rolls of toilet paper and little bottles of shampoo. I stood and considered the vinyl bags that bookended the empty shelves. It certainly wouldn't be the first time I'd found something lurking in a laundry basket. When we were kids, Dewey was always bringing home creepy crawlies that proved to be expert escape artists. It was one of the reasons Mom insisted we find our own digs when we came back to town.

I gave the cart a hard shake and jumped back. The maid squeaked and sprayed me with cleaner.

"Sorry," she said.

I waved away a cloud of ammonia and gave her the look I usually throw at *Dewzers* who try to take my picture.

"Put it down."

The bottle slid from her fingers and clattered on the concrete walkway.

"Now. You grab that side," I pointed at the cart, "and I'll grab this side and we're going to rock it."

After about twenty seconds of wiggling, the cart sprang free taking her side of the door frame with it. The maid started dancing around like she'd run over her foot.

"Are you okay?" I asked.

"I broke the door," she whimpered.

I picked up the strip of twisted metal in my gloved hands and tried to bend it straight. "Maybe we can nail it back in."

She stamped her feet. "I'm too much of a freakin' nice person," she declared loudly.

"O-kay." Why she was throwing out personality traits was beyond me.

"I am, you know," she said. And then she kicked the housekeeping cart a couple of times.

I tossed the metal strip from the door aside and reached for the tongs and their triple coated rubber top jaw that makes them ideal for handling combative species.

"I'm gonna go look inside for the snake," I said. She ignored me and turned her full attention and the heel of her right shoe on one of the poor cart's wheels.

I crossed the threshold for room eleven and did a quick scan. If you ignored the carpet's wall-to-wall stains, it wasn't all that bad. A double bed took up most of the space. The rest was filled by a round table with a single chair in front of the window and a low four-drawer dresser topped by one of those old TVs that are about three feet thick. Off to the right, I could see a toilet through a half-opened door. I didn't spot a suitcase or any personal items but that didn't mean the room was vacant. Checking in without luggage was probably standard practice for a place like this. Travel light and make a quick getaway.

While I poked the tongs anyplace a snake might be hiding, I heard the maid add one of my favorite four letter words to her assault on the cart. I paused for a moment to enjoy it. In a way, it was therapeutic for me too. I really missed saying it.

When I finished my circuit I realized I hadn't seen a trashcan. I did a quick 360 and spotted one in the bathroom, next to the toilet. It was small but who knew just how big the snake really was. I leaned the tongs against the stall shower and dumped the contents of the trash in the sink. Nothing wriggled up out of the tissues and fast food wrappers.

"I think it's gone," I yelled over my shoulder.

The cursing outside stopped.

A moment later, a child-like voice squeaked behind me. "Really?"

I nodded and smiled at the maid's reflection in the mirror above the sink, glad to see that her freak-out was over.

"Really," I said.

And then the screams started all over again.

I followed her line of sight and looked up.

A white snake was draped across the light fixture above me. The maid's use of the word "big" had been an understatement. Its midsection, thicker than my arm, sagged between each of the three bulbs and its face was suspended mere inches above mine. A forked pink tongue flicked in and out as the snake decided its true interest in me.

Blast.

6

A snake can only strike if it's coiled.

Wait. Was that true or was that an old wives' tale? I tried to imagine Dewey saying it. *A snake can only strike if it's coiled.* Instead all I could hear was: *Read my books, June. Watch my show, June. Get eaten by a snake trying to cover for me, June.*

I hated my life.

The snake flicked his tongue at me.

"Same to you," I whispered.

Out of the corner of my eye, I could see the tongs where I'd propped them against the shower. A fat lot of good they'd do me way over there. Oh, who was I kidding? Even if I *could* reach them, my tong-using skills were limited to rescuing fallen socks from behind the washer and dryer. My only hope was to get out of there and lock the giant snake in till reinforcements arrived.

Back up. One foot behind the other. No sudden movements.

I reached for the bathroom door behind me and slammed my funny bone into the knob. A lightening bolt of pain shot up my arm and I made a whole lot of sudden movements. The snake took all this the wrong way and lunged. Before I could scream, the stressed light fixture ripped from the wall and the scaly monster was flung at me.

I threw up my hands to shield my face and somehow caught the snake instead. He was heavier than he looked and I collapsed. My knees hit the tile floor with a loud crack and I cried out as I fell to my side, pinned under the weight. For a moment, we both lay still, stunned from the shock of the fall. Coiled to strike was a wives' tale after all. I decided that if I told Dewey about this later, I'd say I caught the snake on purpose.

Black boots filled my angled view of the open doorway and I looked up.

It was Leather Girl. She'd lost the ripped windbreaker but was still decked out in the black leather ensemble and for some reason she was holding a snake of her own. No. It wasn't a snake. It was a garden hose capped by one of those spray nozzles and it was pointed right at me.

"Wait, don't...."

And then Leather Girl twisted the end and a canon of water shot me across the tile floor. My head smacked into the corner of the stall shower and the tongs fell across my lap.

"Why did you do that?" I yelled.

"It was attacking you," she yelled back.

Not in my version of the story. "It fell. I *caught* it." I held up empty hands. Blast. "Where's the snake?"

Leather Girl stood up on tippy toes and waved the hose around the room. "I don't see it. Why don't I see it? Where'd it go?"

A scream from outside answered that question.

I held out the tongs and Leather Girl yanked me to my feet.

We found the maid on the sidewalk. Her eyes were squeezed shut and she was emptying her spray bottle into the darkness just beyond the edge of the motel. I dug a flashlight out of the orange bucket and waved it over the desert landscape. There was nothing to see but miles of lonely cactus. Cacti. *Cactus?* Either way, how did a snake that size disappear so blasted fast?

"It's gone," Leather Girl said. Like it was a bad thing.

"What are you doing here?" I was starting to feel like she was following me.

"We were finished at..." she glanced over at the maid, who was busy with her spray bottle, and lowered her voice, "...the *place* and Moira radioed that you might need some help."

"That was helping?" I asked. "I had it in my hands. All I had to do was bag it." Assuming I'd have been able to get to my feet. And find a big enough bag. "And why the bath?" I worked my wet hair free of the ponytail holder and squeezed out about a gallon of water.

Leather Girl sidestepped the splatter and tipped her head at the maid. "I get here and she's screaming about a snake." She shrugged and gestured at the pool. "Where there's a pool, there's a garden hose and a good soaking will disarm a perp. I figured it would work on a snake too."

"I could have drowned." I could have. Maybe.

"I figured this was a better option than the rifle in my car."

She had me there.

Beside us, the maid's spray bottle finally ran dry. She threw it at the darkness with a grunt then turned to me. "Can you stick around for a while? He might be mad when he comes back."

She was really losing it if she thought the snake was out there somewhere, plotting his revenge. "I don't think you need to worry. Snakes don't hold grudges."

"I was talking about the guy in room eleven." She shook her head and gave me that look that people reserve for the truly idiotic.

The woman had just coated the desert in ammonia and I was the crazy one? "Right. Sorry. I can't stay." I grabbed my supplies and started for my truck. For some reason, everybody followed, so I sped up.

As I passed room five, the door opened a crack and a male voice hissed from the darkness, "Come here quick."

Without breaking stride, I swung the tongs in that direction.

I'd had enough for one night. "Not now, creep." The door slammed shut.

By room two, the others had caught up.

"Who travels with a snake?" Leather Girl asked.

Off hand, I could think of a couple of dozen people who did. Dewey. The crew at H.A.H. *Morgan.* I stumbled mid-step and froze in place as a wave of nausea washed over me and for a hot second I was in Morgan's front room looking down at my blood covered fingers....

I felt a cool hand on the back of my neck and my head was pushed down toward my knees.

"Breath in through your nose," Leather Girl whispered in my ear. "Let it out through your mouth."

That sounded like a good idea but I was afraid that if I opened my mouth I was going to puke all over her fancy leather boots. I turned my head to one side and the maid's sneakers came into view. One of them tapped furiously.

"So what about the guy?"

Okay, maybe it would be good to puke a little. I opened my mouth but nothing came out. After a moment, the nausea passed and I felt a little disappointed. I waved off Leather Girl and straightened up.

"Well?" the maid asked.

"Just say you opened the door and it slithered out." I cleared a path with the snake hook and resumed my getaway.

When we reached my truck I tossed the bucket and tongs in the back.

"Haven't you been listening to me at all since you got here?" the maid demanded.

Not really. "Sure," I said. "You're a nice person." She'd said it about a dozen times.

"Because I didn't tell the manager that the guy in eleven had animals. I saved him like three fifty-dollar pet fees."

"Okay. You're really nice," I said.

"No," she stamped her foot again. "If he was hiding the

snake, he could be hiding other stuff." She was starting to get that look she'd had when she beat up the housekeeping cart and I wished I still had the tongs in hand.

"Everybody who checks in here is hiding stuff," I said. "That guy back there probably has body parts in his luggage."

"Why would you say that? I have to work here." She moved within kicking range and Leather Girl stepped between us.

"That's enough." Her voice took on a cop tone and she turned to the maid. "If you're worried that the man in room eleven will become violent and blame you for releasing his snake, I can stay." She dug a thin wallet out of a pocket that did not belong in a skirt that tight and flashed a deputy sheriff's badge. "Deputy Lolly Stober."

I almost smacked a hand against my forehead. *Stober*. That was her name.

The maid gave her a good-once over and Leather Girl smoothed that imaginary wrinkle in her skirt again. "I was off duty," she mumbled.

"Great, that's settled." I climbed into my truck's cab and pulled the door shut before they could say anything else.

Leather Girl rapped her knuckles on the window and I reluctantly rolled it down an inch.

"Are you sure you should drive? Maybe I should call a relative?"

That was the last thing I needed. "I'm okay, but hang on... uh...you." I'd forgotten her name again so I just wiggled my fingers and then dug around in the glove box till I found a small tin of business cards. "If you need help finding the snake, call this guy." I passed the card for H.A.H's president out the space at the top of the window. Dewey would never forgive me if he found out that I'd left someone's pet in the desert to fend for itself.

Leather Girl examined the card. "Sammy at hah dot com? Is he funny?"

"Not even a little." I couldn't remember which one he was but I felt safe with that assessment.

"Hey," the maid started patting down her pockets. "Hey, did you see my pass key when you were in room eleven?" She waved a hand at me and I pretended that I couldn't hear her.

"It's on a yellow chain," she added yelling louder.

I shrugged and held a hand up to my ear. Leather Girl knew what I was up to but she came to my rescue anyway. "Let's go have a look," she told the maid.

As they started back across the lot, I threw the truck into gear and gunned the gas. I didn't want to be around when the maid saw what we'd done to the bathroom.

7

It was a little before nine when I pulled up to the sheriff's station. I parked beside a faded old school bus that was hogging most of the spots, and then jogged across the street and down one block to Millsie's. Between the clinic and the snake, I'd killed more time than I'd intended. If mom was at all irked about my disappearing act it would be best to show up with reinforcements, which in her case was a bottle of watermelon water and a double order of Alvaro's extremely disgusting Pukin' Pickle Poppers. Think jalapeño poppers but with tequila soaked dill pickles and wasabi. My mom certainly had an iron stomach cause these babies were guaranteed to ensure the same results as an afternoon of snake hunting with H.A.H.

I'd been about ninety minutes, so chances were really good that Warren had figured out what he needed to figure out and mom and Dewey were long gone. Moira would give me the all-clear and I could still get home in time to be one drink away from passing out in the hot tub before midnight. Tomorrow I'd think about what might have happened to Morgan. Until then, everything had to just be about Dewey.

I pulled open the heavy wooden door of the sheriff's office, expecting to see Moira lean back in her chair, cock an eyebrow and comment about my swim with Moby Dick. Instead, I waded into a sea of noisy chaos decked out in studded black leather and silver chains.

The waiting area for the Horseshoe Bend Sheriff's department was jam packed with metal heads in varying degrees of injury: black eyes, split lips, slinged arms. From the look of things, it had been a colossal fight. Which explained the bus.

Beyond reception, the bloodier individuals were scattered around the four squad room desks where two deputies were trying to get statements and another two were trying to stop an argument without bashing in heads. If Dewey was in a holding cell and any of these people joined him, our little secret was over. When my brother was nervous, he got chatty and I could see him walking someone though the afternoon's events. Warren had promised to be discreet, but I needed Moira to tell me that if Dewey wasn't long gone, he was at least somewhere out of sight. I gave half a thought to slipping around through the back door, but that involved getting past a keypad that I knew Warren changed on a regular basis so I pushed on ahead.

When I'd finally woven my way to the reception desk the face that popped up from behind Moira's computer wasn't Moira.

She might have been my age but it was hard to tell. Heavy black liner circled her eyes and a diamond shaped burst of blue in her jet black hair matched her lips. The rest of her outfit mimicked the crowd, though she was the only one in the room who appeared to be blood free.

"Hang on." She raised a hand covered in heavy silver rings and turned her attention back to the phone cradled on her shoulder. None of the deputies seemed to care that she was in Moira's chair. Or that she had Moira's reading glasses propped on her nose. I squinted my eyes to make sure she wasn't really Moira in disguise.

"Line's back there," a Metal Head leaned into my personal

space and jerked a thumb at the crowd behind us. I considered ignoring him and simply climbing over the little swinging gate that separated reception from the deputies, but after my run-in with the snake, I wasn't sure my knees would cooperate. Since there was no way I was waiting in line, I lifted the bag of poppers and the guy's nostrils did a little dance.

"Trade ya?" I offered.

The grumbler didn't wait to be asked twice and I felt a pang of regret as I watched mom's peace offering disappear into the crowd. With a sigh, I turned back to Fake Moira.

"Unless there's an outstanding warrant, Chief's orders are to turn 'em loose." She grabbed a pen and paper. "How do you spell that?"

The grumbler reappeared. His mouth was too full to ask so he just pointed at the watermelon water that I'd set on the counter.

I shrugged. It wouldn't be the same by itself.

He grinned and then melted into the crowd.

I turned back as Fake Moira rolled the desk chair over to the message cubbies and slid a note into one of the slots.

"Where's Moira?" I asked when she'd returned.

She leaned back in her chair, wiggled a finger at my head and delivered a spot-on imitation of the station's receptionist. "I'm loving what's going on there."

I'd never had anyone compliment my hair before, much less the real Moira. How much stranger could this day get?

"Hang on." Fake Moira held up a hand and then dove into an over-sized satchel that was hanging from the back of the chair. She dug around for a bit and then took my hands and slipped something between them. "That one's still in the testing phase. Let me know what you think."

I looked down at my cupped palms and realized I was cradling one of those little bottles of booze that cost ten bucks from the hotel mini-bar. This one had no label and was filled with a clear liquid. As I turned it over in my hands, I thought I heard her say something about radishes. When I looked up she was back on the phone.

"Horseshoe Bend Sheriff's Station...really?...it'll probably just fly away if you leave it...." After a long pause she choked back a laugh and held the phone to her chest. "There's some kind of bird in her yard and it keeps screaming, *I'm so screwed, I'm so screwed*, at the top of its lungs. Apparently she's afraid this will scar her innocent grandchildren." She scoffed and rolled her eyes. "I can hear the little thugs in the background playing Grand Theft Auto." That sounded more like Moira. She put the phone back to her ear. "Yep, if I had kids and they heard that... let me give you the number for animal control." She cradled the phone again and spun Moira's Rolodex.

As entertaining as my new friend Fake Moira was, I could see that standing here was going to get me nowhere. I dropped the bottle into my purse, wove back through the crowd and took the stairs to the second floor. Most of the government offices for Horseshoe Bend had been housed in the upper levels of the building since a fire gutted city hall in the early 90s. There'd been plans to rebuild, but over time everybody had decided that this was just easier. As I passed the darkened animal control office, I could hear a phone ring.

At the end of the corridor, I took the stairs back down to the first floor and emerged into a dimly lit alcove. I turned away from the exit to the street and considered the forest green door with the words *AUTHORIZED PERSONNEL ONLY* stenciled across the center in red block letters. I stepped up to the keypad I needed to get past.

As kids, Dewey and I had spent plenty of time wandering these halls whenever mom worked a double shift and her coffee buddy was playing babysitter, so I knew that the old Sheriff changed the 6 digit pass code once a week. If Warren had kept up that tradition, that was a lot of numbers to memorize. Chances were good that he was like everybody else in the world and had just a few favorites that he rotated regularly. Maybe some would even be from the old days. All I had to do was start typing in combinations that I remembered and if I was lucky, I'd eventually hit on the right one. My index finger hovered over the keypad and I glanced up at the video camera positioned near the ceiling. Did an alarm go off if you were wrong too many times?

I curled my left hand into a fist and knocked.

It took about five minutes of pounding on the door before Moira appeared.

"Smart girl coming in this way. It's crazy in reception."

I squinted just to make sure it was really her. It was.

"What's going on?" I asked.

"Le Leche Celestial. You should have been here for the hoedown. It's short of impossible to book drunks when they won't stop line dancing."

I had no idea what Le Leche whatever was but she didn't give me a chance to ask.

"Would you get in here, June, before someone sees you."

I didn't tell her about my first stop at reception. It was nice being the smart one for a change.

8

I found Warren in an observation room watching Mom and Dewey through a two-way mirror, his back to the door. Untouched take-out from Millsie's spread out over the table behind him. The sound from the other room was muted but I could tell they were deep into a mom-sided conversation. Her talking, Dewey with his head resting in his hands, listening.

"You know there's a really big crowd out there," I pointed over my shoulder and then dropped my finger. It's not like they were standing right behind me. I caught sight of my reflection in the glass and winced. Fake Moira must have been high. My hair was a disaster that had dried to a mile high frizzy mess. I tried to pat it down and wished for a ponytail holder. Or a really big hat.

"Did you get a hold of Harrison Kim?" Warren asked without turning around.

Blast. I'd completely forgotten about him. Not only had I'd gotten my baby brother arrested but now I was letting him rot in jail. Not accurate, but that was how Mom was going to see it.

"I'm sorry. I forgot. I'll call him right now." I slapped my back pocket and remembered that my cell phone wasn't there. And that I was wearing men's jeans. And that they fit me way too well. "Wait, my cell phone, it's..." I had no idea where it

was. When did I have it last? I called Dewey from my truck...
then walked into Morgan's front room...then I stumbled in the.
...oh yeah.

I'd done such a good job pushing Morgan out of my head,
that I'd almost forgotten about the fact that he was probably
dead. *Don't think about all the blood.*

"You're not going to want your phone back," Warren said.

"Probably not." My stomach gurgled and I let out a long
slow breath. *Don't think about all the blood.* "I'll call from out
front."

"Forget it," Warren said. He was still watching Dewey and
Mom in the little room next door. "Kim's not answering his
phone. My best guess is that he's at the concert."

That made sense. There wasn't much else to do in this town.

"I'm going to check on Dewey," I said.

"Actually, June, come in and sit down." Warren finally turned
to look at me and I gasped. There was a nice sized lump under
his left eye. I touched my cheek and tried to remember just how
hard I'd been swinging when I hit him, in case I ever needed to
inflict that kind of damage again.

Warren mistook my gesture for regret and shrugged his
shoulders. "It was just a lucky shot. You didn't mean it."

I dropped my eyes, ashamed that his welfare hadn't been my
first thought. Warren was too nice a guy. Well, not that nice a
guy. Dewey was still locked up in his jail.

"How's the hand?" he asked.

I looked down at my red knuckles. At the moment, my knees
hurt worse. "I'm okay."

"Okay." He leaned against the two-way mirror and folded his
arms. "Tell me why Morgan didn't go to Costa Rica."

Because there was no way I was going to be stuck in the
jungle for three weeks with Morgan. At the time, I completely
hated him. Right now...I felt conflicted. He *was* probably dead
after all. "He wasn't needed. Can Dewey go now?"

"No." The word felt like a slap in the face.

Warren pushed one of the chairs away from the table with his foot. "Sit."

I was too tired to argue.

"The DA is going to love this case," Warren said. "He's going to see it as open and shut. Your brother was found in a house filled with the blood of his best friend. A man who is currently missing."

I held up a hand. "It's Morgan's blood then?"

"It's the same type," Warren said.

"But it could be anybody."

He considered me for a moment and then a tiny bit of the cop attitude melted. He dug his phone out of a pocket, fiddled with the screen and started reading. "The blood we found is type B negative. It's not common. Depending on the ethnic group, it's in less than two percent of the population."

"But it could still be somebody else?" *Dewey would be inconsolable....*

Warren put his phone away. "We're waiting on DNA tests. Are you okay?"

Was I? I wasn't sure. It was going to take me a while to get used to the idea that I'd never get the chance to yell at Morgan again.

"How long will the DNA tests take?" I had a feeling it was going to be a lot longer than on TV.

"Awhile. Dewey could sit in jail awhile. And in the meantime, the DA will start his public campaign."

"Let me guess," I interrupted. "He's running for office."

"They're always running for office. And this is gonna get him state-wide name recognition. He'll say Dewey and Morgan argued...."

I opened my mouth to protest but Warren raised a hand.

"I've got a witness who says Morgan and Dewey fought the night before the Costa Rica trip. Punches were thrown."

"So. Guys fight sometimes. They argue, they duke it out and then they shake hands and go hunt for snakes." I'd never understood how men could get past an argument so easily. We women knew how to hold a grudge.

Warren cleared his throat to regain my attention.

"The DA will say that the fight caused bad blood between them and that's why Morgan was dropped from the Costa Rica trip."

It was like he was trying to annoy me on purpose. "Morgan was never *on* the Costa Rica trip. He went to Mexico to help out on a b-roll shoot."

"B-roll?" Warren asked.

"The stuff they cut away to in the show when Dewey's talking about other stuff." Three weeks in the jungle with a chatty cameraman-slash-video-editor and I still sounded like an idiot.

"Okay," he said, "but it's not as glamorous as a trip to Costa Rica."

"He was never going to be on that trip. And there's *nothing* glamorous about Costa Rica," I said. At least the part of it that I saw.

Warren began to pace and I had an unobstructed view of the room on the other side of the observation window. Dewey had his head on the table and Mom was rubbing his shoulders. She seemed to be talking in slow motion. Wait. Was she singing? I squinted my eyes. Blast. She was. She was singing to Dewey while he tried to sleep. When I broke my leg, she had me assigned to a different floor at her hospital so it wouldn't look like I was getting preferential treatment. I no longer regretted trading away her pickle poppers.

"June? You still with me?" Warren waved a hand in my face.

"Um, yeah. Wait, no. Morgan not going to Costa Rica was kind of a promotion. He was in charge of the Mexico shoot. Well, it was him and a camera guy, but he was in charge." In the other room, mom started singing a song that was a little more upbeat.

"Okay," Warren said. "So the DA will say that Dewey came home, was still angry over the fight," his hand shot up before I could open my mouth, "he went to Morgan's house to confront him, they fought and Dewey killed him in a fit of rage."

I'd never seen my brother in a fit of anything. He was the most even-tempered person I knew. Probably cause I'd gotten all the angry genes. "So where's the body?" I spit out the words before he could raise a hand.

Warren dropped into the chair across from me and shrugged. Even if he'd have known, I doubt he would have told me. He leaned back and laced his fingers behind his head. It was a smug move that made me want to smack him, and I was pretty sure I knew how hard I'd have to throw the punch to make his eyes match. I let out a breath and sat on my hands. One Nash in the clinker was enough for the moment.

"If Dewey killed Morgan, why was he still in the house?" I asked.

"To clean up and hide the evidence."

"He wasn't hiding anything. He asked me to meet him there." In frustration, I stood up so fast my chair flipped over and hit the floor with a sharp clang. In the other room, Mom paused in the middle of her *do re me* and let her eyes drift over the mirror. I knew she couldn't see us but could she hear us?

Warren tapped the table to get my attention. "Your brother told you, *come now,*" and then he used air quotes, *"your job's at stake."* I'd never seen Warren use air quotes. "He sounded pretty desperate to me."

"How do you know what he said?" I had a feeling I already knew the answer.

"I have your texts."

Of course he had my texts. He had my phone. And Dewey's. Which meant he had access to everything we'd ever sent each other. At least, everything we hadn't deleted. Wait. Could he get a hold of deleted messages too? My mind raced back over the entire life of my cell phone usage and I tried to remember how many times, over the years, that I'd bitched to Dewey about Mom. Had I bitched about Warren? Had we speculated about their coffee sessions? Just how far back could you go into some-one's cell phone history?

"June?" Warren leaned across the table. "I'm not interested in anything that isn't related directly to this case."

So there were a lot of instances. Blast. Okay, don't think about that now. Think about the last thing that Warren said. It was important. Oh yeah, the text. *Come now, your job's at stake.* It had been an innocent statement. "Dewey wanted me at the house so he could show me some stupid baby snakes."

Warren shrugged. "Cover story."

I could feel my fingers itching to form a fist. It was a good thing I couldn't bend them. "Okay, Sheriff Mitchell, why isn't the DA here now, instead of you?"

A smile tugged at the corner of Warren's mouth and for the first time that day I felt some hope. "DA Benge and his wife are currently up in Green Valley for her parent's 60th wedding anniversary. He won't be back in the office until 9 am Monday morning. He'll start his day by having coffee with his niece Lucille." The animal control officer. She was always hanging around Dewey wanting to talk snakes. "He won't be interested in any arrests from the weekend till about 10 o'clock."

"What does that mean for Dewey?"

"That we've got a little over 48 hours to figure out what happened in Morgan's house."

"Without the public finding out," I added.

Warren stood. "Without the public finding out."

Okay. That could work. "So what do we do first?"

"Well, I investigate. You take your mother home."

"And what about Dewey?" I asked.

"For now, he stays here as a person of interest." Warren held open the door and motioned me out into the hall.

"And you'll prove he's innocent," I said.

"I'll find out the truth. Come Sunday night, he'll either be arrested or released." He tried to guide me up the hall toward the back staircase but I dug in my heels.

"Wait. You don't really think he did something to Morgan, do you?" There was no way he could believe Dewey would hurt someone let alone kill them.

Warren frowned. "Sometimes we don't see things that are right in front of us. And when we do they can throw us off balance."

I felt completely numb. He actually thought Dewey was capable of murder. "You think he might have done it."

"June, I've known you and your brother since you were five but that doesn't really mean a thing. Sometimes you only see what people want you to see. I can't let what I think I know about him or you cloud my judgment."

Wait, what did I have to do with this?

"For Dewey's sake, everything needs to go by the book. In a grayish kind of way. For now, he stays here, quietly, until I figure all this out."

On cue, Mom emerged from the little room and I caught a quick glimpse of Dewey, dead asleep and drooling all over the table. She quickly pulled the door shut.

I opened my mouth, ready with an excuse for my extended disappearance but she saved me the trouble.

"I want to leave now, June."

Warren moved to one side to let her pass and though she didn't look at him, I saw their fingertips briefly touch in more than an *I'll see you later for coffee* kind of way. It seemed a lot had happened during my three weeks in the jungle.

9

Mom was quiet on the drive home. Because I don't know a good thing when I'm in the middle of it, I opened my mouth. "So what's up with you and Warren?"

The next twenty minutes were spent listening to an anecdote about two neighbors who shared a fence and a love of astronomy, which somehow led to an ER visit in the middle of the night. Since telescopes were involved, I guessed it all had something to do with minding your own business. I wasn't *completely* sure but I certainly wasn't going to ask for a clarification.

When we got back to her house, Mom was still on point, and kept on talking, as she got out and started up the driveway. I thought about ditching her, but figured she'd just call me to finish the story. I put the truck in park and followed her inside.

She went straight for the kitchen and I kicked off Dewey's boots and sank into the couch. I could hear the unmistakable clunk of ice dropping into a low ball glass followed by crackles and pops as warm Zacapa was poured straight from the bottle. A drink sounded good but I wasn't sure I had enough energy to hold a glass. In the end, she didn't offer, so it didn't matter.

The back blinds were open and I stared out at the lit patio.

Just past the built-in grill and wet bar, a well-worn foot path meandered through the darkness to Morgan's house. In my mind, I followed the twists and turns through the half mile of Prickly Pear Cactus...cacti...*cactus?* Blast. I couldn't completely wrap my head around the idea that he was dead. I ran a finger down the thin scar that cut through my left eyebrow and thought about the last time I'd seen him. There'd been rattlesnakes, lots and lots of rattlesnakes.

"June."

I looked up. I hadn't realized Mom was standing in front of me. Or that she'd stopped talking. "Why don't you just stay here tonight. You've got to drive me back to the hospital for my car anyway. I'll set out sheets in the guest room."

Which was my old room, of course. Dewey's old room was a shrine filled with newspaper clippings, books and the dried snake skins he'd collected over the years. She hadn't changed anything in there since we'd left for college. I probably wasn't as bitter about it as I should have been.

"I love the new article," she called from the other room.

When wasn't there a new article. I found it on the coffee table, carefully torn from a magazine. "Tongs, the ABC's of Safe Use." A full-page photo showed Dewey perched on a ladder, lifting a really big snake off of a curtain rod with the exact same pair of tongs I'd taken to the motel. And there I was stretched out on a couch below them, lost in one of Dewey's books, oblivious to the dangers lurking above me. *Oh yeah.* The magazine had asked me along for a side article on families in show business. That's how I'd found out about the tongs in the first place. The photo shoot had been months ago. I'd completely forgotten.

While Mom started back on her story about the telescope and the fence, I rested my head on the arm of the couch and studied my brother's face in the photo. What was it that Warren had said? *Sometimes you only see what people want you to see.* No. I knew Dewey better than he knew himself. He wasn't hiding anything. He was just oblivious to life. If he'd have been paying attention, he'd have found the blood right away and called 911 and he'd be a witness and not a suspect. When this was all over, I was going to have a heart-to-heart with him. He needed to realize that being so single minded made him miss out on some pretty important stuff. I yawned and tossed the article back on the table without reading it.

~

I woke up to the smell of bacon. I was still on the couch, buried under a quilt that Mom had tossed over me sometime during the night. I was starving but I was pretty sure I'd fallen asleep before the end of her fence story and I was afraid that if she knew I was awake, she'd pick up right where she'd left off, so I lay as still as possible and pretended to be asleep.

"Stop pretending you're asleep, June. It's getting late and we still need to eat before we go."

I sat up and forced a yawn. "Morning. When did you get up?"

"Honestly, June."

I could tell she was deciding which anecdote best fit this situation so I rolled off the couch and staggered up the hall to the bathroom. Along the way, my knees crackled and popped as much as the ice in mom's drink last night. I didn't have to look at them to know they were covered in bruises.

After taking care of business, I caught sight of my reflection in the mirror and gasped at the frizzy mess all over my head. It was worse than yesterday. I longed for a shower but settled for reclaiming my curls with a few splashes of water from the faucet. I had a little trouble getting the fingers on my punching hand to bend so I swallowed a couple of aspirin. Between my knuckles and my knees, all I wanted to do was crawl back into bed.

"Everything is going to get cold, June," Mom shouted from the kitchen.

I added headache to my list of aches and pains and swallowed another pill. "Give me a minute."

I snuck up the hall to Mom's bedroom. I really wanted to get out of Morgan's clothes and who knew when I'd get my suitcase back from Warren's evidence room. In the closet, I stepped around a pile of things that hadn't made it to the laundry basket and a lacy blue bra caught my eye. Why hadn't she been wearing that yesterday when she decided to strip in my truck? I plucked it up and stared at the silky yellow boxers that dangled from a snag on the clasp. Since when did she start wearing *oh my God, they had to be Warren's. I did not need to know that a man's man like Warren wore silky yellow boxers.*

"You have a call."

I spun around to face Mom and tossed everything behind me. "Who is it?" I asked.

"What are you doing in here? I don't have anything that would fit you."

We weren't that much different in size but I let it go for now. "Who's on the phone?"

"Dewey's literary agent."

Blast. *Sarah Sunshine.* He thought she was great but the woman gave me the willies. She was one of those people who always had a sickly sweet smile plastered on her face. All that happiness had to be a cover. I fully expected to one day see her on the news, hanging out of a bell tower with a shotgun aimed at the camera.

"Why is she calling you?" Mom asked.

I shrugged. "How did she even know I was here?"

"She said she's been trying to get a hold of you since yesterday. Did you lose your cell again?"

I knew exactly where my phone was. It was in an evidence box at the sheriff's station.

"Yes," I said. It was easier than explaining why it was covered in blood.

"Oh, June." I could tell she was mentally tabbing that away

for a later discussion. "Do you think she's heard about...you know..." she glanced around as if she was afraid that someone might be lingering near her rack of skirts and overhear us.

"Sarah's in New York," I said. "Who would have told her?" If word had leaked and the world knew that Dewey was a person of interest in Morgan's death, Mom's driveway would have been packed with news trucks and Sarah Sunshine would be the least of our worries.

"Okay." Mom adjusted her scrub top and tucked her hair behind her ears. "Follow me then." I wasn't sure what she had in mind but I faithfully followed.

In the kitchen, Mom sat me at the island, slid the desk phone in my direction and pressed speaker. I hit the mute button.

"Thanks, Mom. I never would have thought of that myself."

I got her patented *we'll revisit that comment later* look. I dropped my eyes and unmuted the phone.

"Sarah?" I asked.

"Hi, June. It's Sarah" For some reason she was always introducing herself to me. It's not like I was constantly forgetting her name. Not after the first few times anyway. "Good Adventures."

I cringed. "Sure." It was way too early to be that cheerful. "How are you, Sarah?"

"I am wonderful," she continued, "now that I've tracked you down. Thank you so much for asking."

Her voice had the eerie cheerful tone of a Christmas bell ringer who'd just gotten that unexpected twenty. I imagined her wide, toothy grin and involuntarily shivered.

"I was beginning to wonder," she continued, "if you'd vanished into thin air."

"No," I said, wishing that was a possibility.

"Well, I'm just calling to make sure you're not standing me up." She gave a little laugh as if the idea of anyone standing her up was ridiculous.

Mom muted the phone. "Are you supposed to be in New York?" she asked.

Without my calendar in front of me, I had no idea what she was talking about. I shrugged and unmuted the phone.

"For what?" I asked.

"Sunday's book signing. You wanted to look over the venue this morning in case any last minute changes needed to be made."

I hit the mute button. "There's a book signing tomorrow."

"I'm not deaf, June," Mom said.

"I'm sitting here in the lobby of the Strand." Sarah Sunshine's saccharine infused words floated up from the phone between us. "It's just the cutest little hotel."

The Strand? That was off I-19. The nut-job was in town.

"Where's the paper?" I asked Mom. She found it on the breakfast nook and I tore through it till I stumbled upon the full-page ad.

The Herpetology Association of Horseshoe Bend presents the Southern Arizona Reptile Show. This weekend only at the beautiful historic Strand Hotel. With Sunday's special guest speaker, Dewey Nash of Roar and Soar Network's number one nature show, Gone Herpin' appearing live and in person at 3pm to read from his new book followed by a special Q & A. Get your tickets today.

"This is a problem," I told Mom.

And it was. If Dewey didn't appear at the appointed hour, there wouldn't just be a room full of disappointed fans, there would be a room full of disappointed fans who liked to tweet. The execs at the Roar and Soar Network paid a lot more attention to social media than I did. They were bound to notice that their biggest star was MIA in his own hometown and I'd start getting phone calls I couldn't answer. Warren needed to know that he didn't have forty-eight hours to figure things out. If he cared about my family at all, he had till the first restless *Dewzers* tweeted their disappointment at 3:01 on Sunday afternoon.

"Why is she telling you about the signing?" Mom asked. "I thought you stayed out of the book side."

"I do."

"June?" Sarah Sunshine's voice purred up at us. "Have you changed your mind since Philly? Hello?"

Mom shot me a quizzical look. "Didn't you get trapped in a broom closet in Philadelphia?"

"A men's room actually."

A few months ago, at a reptile convention in Philadelphia, a rumor had floated around that Dewey had gotten a reptile related tattoo in a region south of his navel and a few rather ambitious fans had decided to sneak backstage for photographic evidence. After a couple of them had begun to live tweet their adventure, we'd been over-run by a horde of *Dewzers* wanting to get in on the action. We'd ended up hiding out in a single stall men's room till we had been rescued by a sympathetic firefighter who happened to be at the convention with a very loud whistle. When we were safe, I'd insisted on better security in the future and Dewey had insisted that we were never in any real danger. The compromise was that I'd get to check for probable escape routes at all future venues. I guess he'd passed that along to Miss Sunshine.

"So," her voice floated up from the telephone speaker. "Have you changed your mind? Are we not meeting at 9:30?"

Mom and I both glanced over at the microwave. It was 9:31. One minute late and Sarah was already tracking me down. She really was a cheerful pain in my....

Mom tapped my arm. "You have to go."

On the phone, Sarah Sunshine cleared her throat. "If you don't mind getting here soon that would be fantastic. My time is limited this morning and I'd like to go over the Pacific Coast tour that will kick off in Las Vegas. I know a mineral show isn't exactly the place you'd expect fans of Dewey's to congregate but you'd be surprised by all the crossover in this type of...." She droned on and I covered the speaker with my hand.

"What do I say if she asks about Dewey?" I was really bad at lying.

"Is she a lesbian?" Mom asked.

And masking surprise. "What?"

"Well, I've seen the way some women conduct themselves around my son. It's shameful. If she's a lesbian, maybe she'll just be happy to see *you*."

I supposed it was a compliment.

"Despite how you look."

And then it was gone. "I want to go to the station and see what's happening with Dewey."

Mom shook her head. "Don't bother Warren. Let him do his job."

"But you're going to go bother him, right?" I asked.

She scoffed. "Of course."

That made me feel a little better. "Make sure he knows where Dewey has to be on Sunday at 3."

"June?" The muffled voice doubled down on the cheerful factor. "Are you still there? Day two in Las Vegas is going to be just as jammed packed as day one. For starters...."

I left my hand over the speaker and we both ignored her voice.

"Just go and make up an excuse for your brother," Mom said. "I'm sure you could be creative if you put your mind to it."

Wow. Two sort of compliments in one day. I almost smiled. And then she tossed the pans of bacon and eggs into the sink.

"What are you doing?"

"There's no time now June," Mom's look said that it was all my fault.

"But breakfast." I pointed for emphasis.

"Oh, don't worry. I'll just grab coffee with Warren."

I must have given her an odd look because she cocked her head and narrowed her eyes at me.

"What?"

I shrugged. "Nothing." There was no way I was going to explain how coffee was Dewey's and my code word for whatever her thing was with Warren.

She considered me for another moment, then grabbed her purse. "Hurry up."

I had the truck halfway to the hospital before I remembered that we'd left Sarah Sunshine on hold. Blast. I considered going back but I didn't want to waste the time. If she left before I got to the Strand, it would be one less thing to worry about.

10

Twenty minutes later, I'd dropped Mom at her car and was pulling into a spot at the historic Strand hotel just off the I-19. A marque on the sign overhead announced the *Southern Arizona Reptile Show Sat & Sun, 8 - 5 Dewey Nash Sunday at 3 No Overnight Lineups.*

The parking lot was pretty empty but that didn't mean anything. The hardcore collectors would have already come and gone, snatching up anything that was rare or unusual. The rest of the day would be filled with families trying to get their kids away from the TV for a few hours. The real crowds wouldn't materialize till a couple of hours before Dewey's talk on Sunday. A security guard wandering nearby slowed down to eye my truck. He was probably there to make sure there were no early stakeouts. Knowing the *Dewzers*, they'd figure out a way around him.

I dug a hat out of the mess on the passenger floor, tucked my hair up inside and pulled the bill down to my eyes. If Dewey's fans were assembling early, I didn't want to be recognized.

There was no sign of Sarah Sunshine in the lobby but knowing her, she was lurking around somewhere. I needed to find her, act like everything was normal and get back to the sher-

iff's station so I could check on Dewey. A sign by the door
welcomed the reptile show in the Mesquite room. That's where
she probably was. I wandered down a couple of corridors till I
found the place and poked my nose inside.

About a hundred tables were laid out in long rows and
vendors were hawking everything you never knew you needed
for creepy crawlies that climbed, burrowed, slithered or glided
through the air, including the crawlies themselves. For the first
time since all this had started, I was actually happy that Dewey
was locked up in a jail cell. If he'd been here, we'd have had to
stop at each and every table so he could impart some piece of
reptilic wisdom on me.

A twenty-something girl selling tickets from a table by the
door looked up from her cell phone. "You need a ticket to go in."
She sounded almost apologetic.

"I just need to look for someone I'm meeting," I said. I braced
a hand on the door frame, leaned into the room and craned my
neck to peek around a table selling wax worms. A brightly-
colored sign billed theirs as the tastiest around and I was almost
hungry enough to see if that was true. I felt a tug on my sleeve.

"Admission is only six-fifty," Ticket Girl said, "and a portion
of the proceeds helps with educational programs for the public.
But you should really get a two-day ticket," she said. Then she
sighed. "Dewey Nash will be here tomorrow." Her last words
oozed the same way mine did when I talked about pistachio
baklava and Vin Diesel movies.

Just for fun, I scrunched up my face. "Who?"

The girl held her cell phone out in my direction. Her screen
saver was a photo of Dewey. He was signing an adoring *Dewzer's*
t-shirt with a big grin on his face. And there I was, a few steps
away, giving the stink eye to a couple of fans who had gotten a
bit too close. It had a publicity shot feel to it but it could have
been taken by someone at a convention. I lifted Ticket Girl's
hand a bit higher for a better view. My hair looked really good.
For a change. I was tempted to ask for a copy.

"Isn't he adorable?"

My eyes drifted from my soft perfect curls to Dewey's smiling face. I nodded. He was really in his element when he was surrounded by his fans. I didn't want to think about how he probably looked right at this moment. Had Warren put him in one of those orange prison jumpsuits? Did the Horseshoe Bend Sheriff's department use orange prison jumpsuits? Part of me felt like I needed to call Mom and find out but most of me really didn't want to know. Best to file thoughts of Dewey away with those graphic visions of dead Morgan.

I handed back the phone. "Never heard of him." Ticket Girl's jaw dropped and I jerked a thumb over my shoulder. "Is there a snack bar in there?" I asked.

She could only nod.

I tossed a ten on the table and left the poor girl with her mouth dangling open. I sidestepped a family with about a dozen children under ten, wove through the vendor's tables, and headed for the back.

Despite the fact that it wasn't even nine in the morning, the snack bar menu was limited to hot dogs, hamburgers and nachos. I chose a dog with mustard and a bottle of spring water. While I waited for them to put my order together, I leaned against the counter and studied the room. No sign of Sarah Sunshine. And only a handful of window shoppers were wandering the aisles. Most of the vendors looked bored. At the far end, a few were hovering just outside of a door they'd propped open, smoking cigarettes. How had H.A.H. managed to talk this many people into setting up tables? Then I noticed three ladies north of sixty, taking selfies with a giant poster of Dewey. Of course he'd be the draw. The vendors knew that tomorrow a horde of die hard fans would swarm the place and in their fevered frenzy, they'd buy up everything in sight. A slow Saturday was worth the wait.

As I continued to watch the ladies, one of them raised her eyes from the phone they were huddled around and looked directly at me. Uh oh. Had I just been spotted? I'd like to think that no one would look at this outfit and think, dang that's probably June Nash in those man jeans and ball cap. The lady continued to stare and I felt a knot start to form in the pit of my stomach. While I had no problem hissing at most of the *Dewzers* that intruded into my personal space scratching around for a piece of my baby brother, I didn't think I could hiss at a woman my nana's age. Maybe the lady wasn't really looking at me. Maybe she just had a hankering for a dog and a coke. I *was* standing in front of the snack bar and despite the fact that the hot dogs were the cheapo ones and probably just boiled to this side of warm, they smelled delicious.

After what felt like an eternity, the old lady dropped her eyes and I let out a breath. She was just looking at the snack bar menu. My number was called and I stepped over to the pickup window to grab my food. When I turned around, Nana Dewzer was looking at me again. Then she bumped a shoulder against one of her friends and tilted her head in my direction. This went on till all three of them were staring at me while trying to make it look like they weren't staring at me. Blast. I tucked the dog and water into my purse and decided it was a good time to test drive possible escape routes.

I speed walked to a gap in the tables and then cut a diagonal across the space, weaving in and around vendors and calling out apologies as I aimed for an accordion partition that divided the room. Hopefully, the trio on my tail would decide that I was by myself and leave me alone. I glanced back. Nope. They were in hot pursuit. As I got closer to the partition, the words on a large sign came into focus; *Dewey Nash Lecture Sunday 3pm. Open Seating begins Sunday 10am.* I wondered what poor sucker would be entertaining the salivating crowds till my brother showed up. A photo of Morgan came into focus, along with a blurb promising an informative pre-show lecture. Blast.

Had I just slowed down to read that sign? I glanced back. Yep. Nana Dewzer and her gang were about to close the gap and

I could see her taking in a breath, readying to pelt me with requests for things I didn't want to know that nanas thought about. I quickened my step and as I turned back toward the partition, bam! I slammed my thigh into the booth for one of the convention's most popular vendors: Rodent Universe.

If you've never seen them at a convention, picture two tables, about three feet apart, covered with long wide bins that are about six inches deep. Now imagine a five-inch wide wire mesh bridge that spans the gap. Oh and add in dozens of little white mice scurrying from one bin to the other and back again. They're always a crowd pleaser.

My collision with the table sent the mesh bridge into a swinging frenzy and workers scrambled as dozens of furry rodents lost their grip and dropped to the floor below. As luck would have it, all the mice ran straight for the old ladies who shrieked and scattered.

Thankfully, there were several small children in the vicinity, so I was spared the choice words that usually accompany the kind of looks the Rodent Universe gang were throwing my way.

I picked up speed despite my new limp and slipped around the edge of the partition only to find myself face to face with the biggest macaw I'd ever seen in my life. Perched on a hunk of wood at the end of a table stacked with pamphlets, the bird twisted its face to study mine, shook its red feathers and screamed, "AWK, I'm so screwed!"

I knew the feeling.

"June?" A woman in a baggy jumpsuit twisted her head just like the bird had and grinned at me. How did people keep recognizing me in this outfit?

"How are you? Welcome back to town."

I glanced at the name embroidered on the breast pocket. Blast. It was Lucille, the DA's niece. The one person in the whole world that I wanted to avoid. Besides Sarah Sunshine. And any random *Dewzer*, of course.

My brain screamed run but my feet refused to move.

"Shouldn't you be in Green Valley?" I asked. Blast. Should I know about that? Too late. "Congratulations on your grandparent's sixtieth anniversary."

Her grinned broadened. "Thanks. We're so proud of them." Then she leaned toward me and lowered her voice, "They hate each other's guts but they'll stand together for photos, so that's nice."

I had no idea how to respond to that so I pointed at the bird. "What's up with him?"

The macaw stretched its neck and snapped at the air in front of my finger. I quickly jammed my hands into the safety of Morgan's deep pockets. When all this was over, I was keeping these jeans.

"He's an odd duck, isn't he?" Lucille said.

For half a second I thought she was talking about Morgan. Then she made kissy sounds at the bird and it ruffled its feathers and wiggled his head in an endearing kind of way. If you liked that sort of thing.

"I rescued him from a yard over near Bishop Street," Lucille said.

"I think I saw him yesterday." Unless there were other giant macaws roaming the streets of Horseshoe Bend, this was the bird from Morgan's yard. And the intersection where I'd nearly driven my mom into oncoming traffic.

"Well..." I continued. I bobbed my head in an *I'm done talking to you and I'm going to leave now* kind of way and took a step to my left. Lucille didn't get the message.

"I'm just holding Rojo, that's what I've been calling him, you know, that's Spanish for red," she said.

"Oh," I said. I bobbed my head again and took another small step.

"Shaun's going to bring me a cage. They've got a booth there today. You remember Shaun Harwood, right?" Lucille asked.

I scrunched my face up trying to remember anyone from my past name Shaun. No one came to mind.

"He had that cool '57 Chevy Nomad."

That jarred things loose and I nodded. I remembered him well. The guy had stood me up for a party when I was a lowly high school sophomore. Dewey and Morgan had retaliated by filling his beloved classic car with hissing cockroaches.

"He's with Fish and Game now," Lucille said. Absentmindedly, she set her cell phone on the table and Rojo sidestepped in that direction. "You should stick around. Shaun'll be by any second."

I was pretty sure he wouldn't be happy to see me. "Oh, I don't really have time...."

"So what are you up to?"

Besides trying to get away from you? "Just checking out escape routes." And not finding any. "In case the crowd's wild tomorrow." My eyes focused on a bright red exit sign in the distance behind her head. The door beneath it was propped open and I could see out into the parking lot.

"Hey, there's one. Nice." I glanced around the space. It was about as big as the tabled area I'd just escaped and had a couple hundred folding chairs crammed together with a long narrow walkway down the center that led to a small elevated stage. There was no greenroom area, but that wouldn't be a problem. We could wait in my truck out in the parking lot, and go in when Dewey was announced. Though, the *Dewzers* would probably count on me doing that. I had a vision of a hundred fanatics rocking my truck trying to shake my brother loose so they could chew on his bones.

"...Not that I'm envious, you know what I mean?"

Blast. What was she talking about?

"Going all over the world getting to really sink his teeth into some pretty amazing creatures."

Oh, Dewey's show. "Yeah. He likes it."

"Some of that stuff he does, like that frog with fangs in New Guinea, weird, but I wouldn't say no to something that wasn't so routine." She leaned in a bit closer. "You know, something *I* could really sink my teeth into." She snorted a couple of times and I decided that I didn't like the way she was looking at me. Where those snake tongs still in my truck?

"Are you okay? You seem kinda jittery. Is Dewey with you? Maybe I should call him." Lucille reached for her cell phone and Rojo pecked her hand.

And then just like in the movies when the hero is saved to a rousing chorus of angels, Sarah Sunshine stepped in the door from the parking lot and sing-songed across the way to us. "June, oh Junie." She was dressed all in peach with the strap for a white leather briefcase slung over her shoulder.

I'd never been so excited to see someone I disliked so much.

"June, it's Sarah. Dewey's book agent," she said as a perfectly manicured hand waved in my direction.

"Every single time," I muttered to myself. "Well, it was great talking to you." I turned to Lucille but she was busy tending to a bleeding finger. I gave Rojo a wide berth and raced to meet Sarah Sunshine halfway.

I tolerated a hug and let her guide me through a glass door that I hadn't noticed before and into a carpeted hall.

"Good Adventures." She waved a fist in the air.

"Sure," I said.

"I'm so glad I found you." Sarah Sunshine took point and I followed at half speed. "No Dewey today?" She glanced back over her shoulder and offered me a view of about three dozen of her teeth.

"He's in hiding," I said. In a way he was.

"I don't blame him. The *Dewzers* are very excited for this talk. Lots of chatter on the web," she said.

I felt a tightness in my chest. Had word leaked out? "What kind of chatter?" I asked.

She glanced back at me and patted her behind. Her pleated skirt was so tight, her hand bounced right off. "The usual nasty kind that really drives book sales. It's better if I don't talk to you about that sort of thing," she added with a wide grin and a wink.

I grimaced. For once, I completely agreed with her.

"We're just up here on the left," she pointed up the hall. "Your reptile group, H.A.H. is it? They were so sweet to give us one of their rooms," She slowed to a crawl and began to dig around in her purse. "If I can find that silly key we can sit down for a minute. I have a few things on my list that we need to go over...."

I opened my mouth to ask just how many things constituted *a few things* but before I could get out a word, a door beside us popped open and a hand reached out. Fingers closed in on my sleeve and I was yanked off my feet and into a room where I tripped over a stack of newspapers and landed on my hands and knees. I twisted around and got a quick glimpse of Sarah Sunshine, still out in the hall searching for her keys. And then the door swung shut. When I turned back, I found myself looking up at a wild-haired bearded homeless guy. I sucked in a deep breath to accommodate the scream that I intended on throwing at him and his eyes widened in fear.

He held up one hand while the other ripped the beard away from his chin. "Ow, ow, ow."

When he was finished, I stared in complete shock at the naked face above me.

It was Morgan Freakin' Durgan.

11

Three liters. That's how much blood Warren had said was in that room. And not just any blood. Type B Negative blood. So rare, it had to be Morgan. *And yet...* here he was, standing in front of me shaking a newspaper in my face. I was hallucinating. I had to be.

"How come I'm not in any of these?" he asked.

I reached out and poked his knee with my index finger. My vision felt very solid.

"Was it on TV at least?" He tossed the paper aside and scratched at bits of beard that still clung to his face. "Local is okay. National would be great. June?"

Was I being punked? I glanced around the room. I didn't see a lot of storage space for hiding jokesters ready to spring out and yell *gotcha*. There was no one under the bed. A couple of suitcases had been dumped out on the floor of the coat closet but the pile didn't look big enough to cover even a kid. Over at the eat-in kitchen all the cupboards were tiny and above the sink. To my left, an open slider revealed most of a fenced-in patio where a couple of empty brown wicker chairs were set around a square picnic table covered with tipped beer cans and overflowing ashtrays. Maybe they'd already had the party.

*Or...*maybe there was a hidden camera. It wouldn't be the first time that Morgan had tried to make me look bad. I lifted my eyes to the ceiling. *Ting, ting, ting.* Nothing up there. Just a ceiling. *Ting, ting, ting.* And a few cobwebs in the corner. *Ting, ting... what was that noise....?*

I dropped my eyes and caught sight of my hallucination-slash-Morgan carrying a silver bucket with the logo for the hotel engraved on it. With each step there was a noisy *ting, ting, ting.* He stopped a foot away and drew the bucket to his side. Wait, was he going to...? And then his arms swung my way. I had just enough time to raise my right hand before a bunch of ice cubes bonked me on the forehead and a wave of cold water washed down my sleeve.

"Morgan!" I shrieked as the icy water pooled around my waist.

"And she's back." He made kissy noises and a skinny streak zoomed in from the patio, then began to zip around the perimeter of the room.

"That's Cyrano," Morgan said. "Don't worry, her spurts only last a few minutes. She's really a big couch potato."

"Roooo....rooo...rooo," the dog sang.

"Shhh." Morgan caught her and clamped a hand down on her muzzle. "Shhhh." When he let go, she went back to racing around the room and Morgan went to the dresser. He set the ice bucket down by the TV and flipped the lid off a cardboard box. After staring at the contents for a long moment, he dumped a stack of fliers for the reptile show by his feet and began to rummage through the dresser drawers.

The spud finished a few dozen circuits of the room then strolled over and leaned against my shoulder. Her long Greyhound tongue uncurled from her mouth and she slapped it in the direction of my face a couple of times. She missed completely but that didn't seem to bother her. As I patted her sides, her ears went into high alert mode and her shiny black nose bounced on the end of its muzzle. Aside from the animation, she looked exactly like every statue of Anubis that I'd been forced to admire when Dewey had dragged me all over Egypt our last summer before college.

Cyrano's nose bounced a couple more times then she wiggled till I let go and she dove head first into my purse. Her long thin tail whipped itself into a frenzied circle and I knew she'd found my hot dog. My stomach growled in protest but Cyrano ignored it.

"My hot dog," I shouted at Morgan.

He shrugged. "Don't put stuff on the floor. That's her domain."

"But...my hot dog."

Morgan sighed and ripped the haphazard wig off his head revealing wiry brown hair that looked just as wild. "Why didn't you call me back?"

I scooped up a cube of ice by my foot and threw it at his face. "You're supposed to be dead."

"Yeessss." He jabbed a fist in the air. "Was it on TV? Because it wasn't in the paper."

"What is wrong with you?" Maybe he *did* hate Dewey. Maybe they *had* fought. Maybe Dewey *had* killed him. *Wait.* None of that happened. Hunger was making me lose my mind. That and the fact that I was talking to a dead man. I needed to call Warren.

"I have to call Warren," I said. There was a phone on the bedside table.

"Why?" Morgan clapped his hands together in a pleading gesture. Cyrano's tail whipped around again and I leaned out of harm's way.

"Because Dewey's in jail you moron," I yelled at him.

"Oh my God, what happened?"

I wanted to flick him in the forehead but he wasn't close enough. "He killed *you.*"

"What?" Morgan turned a pasty shade of white and dropped onto the edge of the bed.

I scrambled to my feet, stepped around the Greyhound sticking out of my purse and grabbed the telephone receiver.

"Warren found him in your house of blood." But it was okay now. Dewey was going to be okay. Morgan was alive. I don't know how considering how much blood he'd left all over his front room floor, but he was alive. I wiped a strand of hair out of my eyes and tried to focus on the telephone keypad. The nine kept coming and going. Blast, I needed food.

"June." Morgan enunciated each word as if he wasn't sure I'd understand. "Why was Dewey in my house?"

"Because you texted him." I shut one eye and the nine came into focus. I pressed it and looked for the one. It was probably somewhere near the two. As soon as Warren answered the phone, I was going to hand it to Morgan and head straight to the hotel dining room and order whatever breakfast platter they had. And then some pancakes. And then maybe a banana split.

"I didn't text Dewey." Morgan dug his phone out of a back pocket. "Wait." He held up a hand then fiddled with the screen. "No...no...no...no. That text was supposed to go to Shaun."

"Fish and Game Shaun?" I asked. My finger hovered over the keypad. Had I pressed the one yet?

Morgan fiddled with his phone some more. "No, no, no." He held out the screen for me to see but it was too far away so I ignored it. "Dewzer and Douche, it's an easy mistake." And then he tapped away at the phone again. "None of these were supposed to go to Dewey. It was supposed to be that ass-hat. He was supposed to knock on the door. He was supposed to go in. He was supposed to fall in the blood. He was supposed to scream like a little girl."

"This was a practical joke? You're still such a jerk! Why does Dewey hang around with you?" I wanted to throw the desk phone at him but it was plugged into the wall. I dropped the receiver and threw my hat instead. "I fell in the blood." And a pen from the nightstand. "I screamed like a little girl." And then a few ice cubes that were melting on the floor. "I had to spend an entire day with my mother." The phone was still attached to the wall but there was more ice around my feet. "And now my baby brother's in an orange jumpsuit and my Mom is singing to him."

"Hey, stop it," Morgan yelled.

I lobbed the last cube and it bounced off his nose. My hands felt too empty so I looked around for something else to throw.

"June, wait," Morgan snagged a pillow from the bed and clutched it like a shield.

The lamp on the bedside table caught my eye.

"You did get my texts right?" he asked.

The ornate base looked heavy but that didn't mean that it was.

"June, are you listening to me?"

"Huh?" I was too busy trying to yank a cord free from the wall.

Morgan raised his voice. "Did you get my texts?"

"What? When?" Success. I slipped two hands around the lamp's base and lifted it easily. *Hey, that ice had really helped my stiff fingers.*

"I texted you a bunch. The last one was right after you signaled me outside of Millsie's."

"I didn't signal you outside of..." my words trailed off as I flashed on yesterday. "The beat up little Honda?" I asked. He nodded. I'd gone up to my office via the dark creepy stairs that I hated just to avoid that driver. Blast. "I wasn't signaling you, I was shielding my face. I thought you were a Dewzer." Now I felt nauseous. And not just from a lack of food. If I'd been paying attention, this would have all been over hours ago. "Wait, you said the last text. When was the first text?"

"After you dissed me at the Cactus Rose," he said.

"You were not at the motel." He wasn't.

"I was. And then that crazy lady started screaming about Strawberry Margarita so Cyrano and I had to hide out in another room." He dug a yellow cord out of a pocket and shook the key at me. *Hey, it was the passkey the maid had lost.* "Think I can just drop this in a mailbox?"

"You were the creepy guy at the motel." I needed something else to throw.

"So you really didn't get any of my messages?" Morgan didn't just sound disappointed. He sounded afraid. And he was right to be. As soon as I got some food in me, I was going to kick his ass.

"I never got any stupid messages," I hissed at him. "My phone is covered in your practical joke blood and it's probably in some evidence box at the sheriff's station." Wait. Evidence. That was important for some reason. "Oh. Oh...oh...." I held up a hand and Morgan lifted the pillow up to shield his cheekbones. "If Warren's got my phone and you texted me, he knows this is all a practical joke."

"This isn't a practical joke," he said.

"Dewey's going to be okay." If Morgan sent me texts last night, Warren would have read them. He'd probably already let Dewey go. No one could reach me because I didn't have my cell. I needed to call Mom. I held up a hand. "Wait." That didn't seem right. I was with Mom till an hour ago. I set down the lamp and leaned against the bedside table to think. "Warren said he had *my* texts. He didn't say anything about *your* texts." Blast. "Warren read my *replies* to Dewey's messages on Dewey's phone." I couldn't believe it. We were right back were we started. "No one knows you're alive."

"Yeessss." Morgan did the fist pump thing again and I picked up the lamp again.

"Wait. June." Morgan lowered his pillow shield. "Look. I'm in serious trouble here. I have to stay dead. At least for a while." He snagged a dog leash off the bed. "Just give me twenty-four...."

I held the lamp a bit higher.

"...ten hours. I'll take a video with you right now." He fiddled with his phone then turned it to his face. "Hey, Warren.

It's me, Morgan Durgan. I'm alive. Dewey didn't kill me. Here's June." He turned the phone to me and then back to his face again. "Yeah, she's pretty pissed. Thanks for not looking for me for a little bit. I'll explain soon and if I don't," he shrugged, "it won't matter." Then he fiddled with the screen some more. "Now, it's set to send to Warren at six am...." He yanked Cyrano out of my purse. Her face was covered in mustard and the receipt for my breakfast. "...Dewey'll be off the hook. It'll all be good."

"You want Dewey to spend another night in jail?" I aimed the lamp at his face.

He glanced down at his wristwatch. "I'm out of time. I have to get out of here right now," he pleaded.

"Not till you talk to Warren." I looked down at the desk phone and punched 9-1-1. A high pitched warble screeched out of the receiver and a robotic voice scolded me, "Your call cannot be completed as dialed. Please hang up and try your call again."

"I'm so screwed." Morgan's voice sounded really far away.

Wait. Who said that recently? I looked up as the door swung shut.

I clutched the receiver unsure of what to do. Morgan was getting away. Would Warren believe that I'd seen him? That I'd talked to him? Would the video really reach him tomorrow at six am? Morgan's message-sending track record wasn't so hot. I dropped the telephone's handset back into the cradle, scooped up my purse and took off after them.

In the hall, I caught sight of Cyrano's tail as it rounded the opposite corner. I raced to the end, turned left and it happened again. One more hall and one more tail sighting and I had to bend over to catch my breath.

"June?"

I peered over my shoulder. Sarah Sunshine was watching me from the other end of the hall.

"June, it's Sarah. Where did you wander off to?"

"Sarah...." I paused to gulp in a few mouthfuls of air.

"911...Morgan." I raised a hand to point at the end of the hall where I'd last seen the Greyhound tail but my wet sleeve kept me from extending my arm. In frustration, I ripped at the fabric till I'd peeled the gingham shirt off over my head.

Sarah eyed the curvy silhouette on my t-shirt and her happy lips drooped into a frown. "Oh, thank God. I'm so glad you realized that outfit is hideous. Go shopping, we'll go over schedules later." With that, she turned on her heels and used a key card to let herself into a room.

I sucked in a couple of breaths. "You're fired."

And then I took off after the disappearing dog tail.

I wasn't in the mood for anymore running so I took the first exit I found. Morgan's car was probably parked someplace inconspicuous for a quick getaway. I'd find it and wait for him to show up. I blinked in the bright sunshine and jogged around the outside of the building till a big green dumpster came into view. Beside it was the beat up little Honda. The passenger door was open and there was Morgan, crouched down beside his Greyhound, his hands a few inches above her back. I'd caught them just in time. He was about to pick her up and toss her in. You had to do that cause apparently the poor thing was clueless when it came to understanding how a four-legged creature is supposed to climb into a vehicle. That's all Morgan had talked about in his last Christmas card. Not that I read it on purpose. Dewey had taped it to the freezer and that's where the ice cream lived.

"Don't... you...dare...." I pointed a finger at them and slowed down to gulp in some air. "Dewey...is...your... best...friend...."

His eyes widened and darted from mine to the service road behind me.

"There's...no...escape...I'm...gonna...kick...your...ass...." I held up a hand. "Hang on." After a few good deep breaths I felt much better. "This is...Dewey we're...talking about."

Morgan did a weird thing with his lips.

"What...is...your...problem?" Another deep breath and most of my lung power felt like it was back. I moved in closer and wagged a finger at him. "He's sitting in a jail cell thinking his best friend is dead and what happens come Sunday afternoon when his forty-eight hours are up? If Warren arrests him, it's going to be all over the news. Roar and Soar is going to cancel the show. His agent is going to drop him. And if he has no show, he won't need an assistant and I'll be out of a job and all my money is tied up in bonds that I can't cash without penalties and fees and I'll have to move in with my mother." And that was the scariest thought of all. "You are going back to town with me, right this minute."

Morgan did the thing with his eyes again and I'd had enough. "Oh screw you." My fingers curled and I was throwing the punch before I knew that I was going to do it. My fist made contact with his chin, he dropped to the ground out cold and I did a little *I've broken my knuckles and I want to cry* dance.

"Nice."

I spun around and was instantly pissed at myself for not noticing the evil looking guy with the gun, lurking in the shadows of the dumpster. He stepped into the sunlight and scratched at the dirty blonde stubble on his chin.

"I think he was trying to warn you about me," he said.

"Yeah," I nodded. "I see that now."

12

"**S**ince my hands are full, you mind tossing him in?" Evil Looking Guy bobbed his head to the left and I leaned around his gun to look into the popped trunk of a black fin-tailed behemoth parked behind him. How had I not seen that either? Oh yeah, I was distracted by the idea of killing the idiot sprawled out around my ankles.

"I'm not sure he'll fit." I didn't want to encourage something that I knew wasn't going to end well.

"Oh, it'll easily hold two," Evil Looking Guy said with a grin.

Uh oh. Even Cyrano whimpered.

All the anger I'd been chewing on earlier was gone and I could feel a pitch in my stomach that was about to turn into a full-blown panic attack. I needed to keep my cool if I wanted to get out of this alive. I dug my fingernails into the palms of my hands and took a quick look around. Of course there was no one in sight. Where was that security guard that I'd seen when I'd pulled into the parking lot? Surely, he checked this area once in a while. This was a perfect spot for a few of the hardcore *Dewzers* to hide out in while they waited for tomorrow's lecture.

"You looking for the security guard? He's busy chasing after some weirdos who were trying to set up a tent between the dumpster and the recycling bin."

Oh yeah. There was a recycle bin too. If I lived through this, Morgan owed me a vacation. Something exotic. With fruity drinks. And lots of sandy beaches. Did I still have a bathing suit that fit? I suppose I could buy something once I got *there*. Wherever there was.

Evil Looking Guy waved the gun at me like he was expecting something. Wait. Did he just ask me a question?

"Huh?" I said.

"Putting up a tent here. You think it's weird?"

Even if I didn't, why would I disagree? I nodded. "It's weird."

"Yeah," he said, "it is."

Were we far from the lecture hall where Lucille was waiting for Shaun? Would she hear me scream? She had been near an open door. If nothing else, she'd probably hear me getting shot.

"We haven't got all day." Evil Looking Guy waved his gun at Morgan. "Just drag him by the shoulders. You should be able to lift and roll him in. It's all about leverage."

I eyed the gun that was motivating me to comply. A couple of breaths settled my stomach and then I slipped my arms under Morgan's shoulders and dragged him backward till I bumped into the car.

After some lifting, shoving, several smacks of his head against the tail lights, and finally bending his knees, I got Morgan into the trunk. And Evil Looking Guy was right. He fit. And yep, there was still plenty of room for me. I considered Morgan's limp body. Blast. I wasn't sure which bothered me more. The fact that I might have killed him or that I could be next.

"You know, you can have him," I said. Chances were really good that he was on one of the hotel security cameras. That was probably all Warren needed. "I won't tell a soul. You saw me yelling. I'm too mad at Morgan to care what happens to him."

The sad part was that in a teeny tiny way, it was kinda sorta true.

His lips curled into a small smile. "Get in."

If I got into that trunk, I knew that there was no way I was getting out on my own and no one would miss me. Mom thought I was meeting with Sarah. Sarah thought I was shopping and Dewey had issues of his own. I really needed some friends who worried about me when I didn't text them all the time. If I got out of this alive, I was going to find some. Right after my Morgan-sponsored vacation. And after I'd caught up on everything at the office. And maybe after February when the show was on hiatus. It was probably a better idea to wait until I wasn't so busy.

The Greyhound whimpered and I looked over at her. *Wait a minute.* Maybe Cyrano could save the day. The news always seemed to be filled with stories about dogs leading cops to half-frozen children and lost old people. If I distracted Evil Looking Guy, would the Greyhound be smart enough to go get help? I caught her eye and she answered my question with a yawn and a belch.

Blast.

"What about Cyrano?" I asked. "We can't just leave her here. She might get hit by a car."

The guy made kissy noises and crouched down as Cyrano ran over to him. Being the lover that she is, she flapped her tongue at the air near his face and then went over to his car, ready for her ride.

Traitor, I thought.

Evil Looking Guy opened the door and she twisted her head to look up at him.

"You have to help her in," I said.

"Is that what the idiot was doing when I pulled up?" Evil Looking Guy asked. He moved to one side and waved his gun at the car. "You do it."

I brushed off all the dirt I'd covered myself in after dragging

Rag-doll Morgan around and knelt down beside his hound. "I guess your daddy's a good guy after all. He wouldn't leave you." I was gonna give her a kiss but her wet black nose was dripping so I just patted her on the head. She dropped her jaw to pant and I waved away her warm, hot dog breath. "If you'd have just done the Lassie thing, you could have been a hero," I whispered.

"Just put her in," Evil Looking Guy yelled at me.

"I am," I yelled back.

I closed my eyes for a second trying to remember the mechanics involved with getting Cyrano in a car. Morgan had been very descriptive in that Christmas letter.

"Today please," Evil Looking Guy said.

My eyes snapped open and I glared at him for a moment. "O-kay."

I lifted Cyrano's front paws and put them up on the seat. She twisted her head and fussed at me. It wasn't quite a bark or a whine. More of a *roooo*. I wondered if she had any idea of the seriousness of the situation. Another roo told me no. She just wanted her ride.

I scratched her neck and then went around to her back legs, picked them up and walked everything forward till she was a ball of hound. I waited for her to do the rest on her own but she didn't seem to know enough to do the rest on her own so I gave her a gentle shove and she sprang forward into the car.

"You need to open a window for her so she can hang her head out and sniff," I said. I hadn't read anything about that in the letter but it seemed appropriate.

"Okay, I'll do that." Evil Looking Guy motioned to the trunk. "Now, get in."

I just couldn't do it.

He took a step toward me. I took a step back and whacked my head on the latch of the open trunk. I clutched at my throbbing skull, twisted an ankle, stumbled on the edge of my boot and fell back in on top of Morgan. I pried my face off his flip flops and twisted till I could see sky.

Evil Looking Guy leaned in. "You okay?"

The gun wasn't in my face anymore so I screamed. That freaked out my kidnapper who cursed and slammed the trunk lid shut. I blinked in the darkness and kept screaming. The engine roared to life, the radio cranked to high and Cyrano howled to the heavens. Rag-doll Morgan and I were tossed around the spacious trunk through a few sharp turns and then rolled into one mess as we zoomed from nothing much to full-speed ahead. I guessed that we were on the I-19 headed to wherever it was easy to dump bodies. The image of becoming vulture bait on an isolated strip of desert made me pump up the volume on my screams till I realized that with all that racket coming from the front of the car, there was no way anyone was going to hear me, so I gave up.

A beam of light cut through the blackness and blinded me.

I raised a hand to shield my eyes. "Cut it out."

"Sorry," Morgan pointed the light at a spot beside my head. "You stopped screaming so suddenly, I thought maybe something had happened to you."

"You mean something besides being kidnapped?" Eventually, the car was going to stop and Evil Looking Guy didn't seem like the type who ended things with a handshake and a promise to keep in touch. An image of him showing up on my doorstep with a bunch of wildflowers popped into my head. That led to giggles which led to snorts which led to a bout of pathetic wheezing, and I felt something warm squish the sides of my mouth together. I opened my eyes.

Morgan had wiggled around to face me and one of his hands was making me do fish lips.

"Vhat a ell rr oo ooing?"

"You're hyperventilating," he said. "It helps if you breathe like you're blowing out a birthday candle."

I bent an arm and tried to slam my elbow into his chest. From two inches away it didn't work all that well, so I just wiggled and kicked my feet.

He let go and I wiped my mouth on the back of my hand.

"I thought I killed you," I said.

He actually laughed. "Come on June, you've got a pretty good right, but seriously."

"You weren't moving. I had to stuff you in this stupid trunk."

"I was playing dead. I thought maybe the guy might just leave if you couldn't pick me up." He rubbed the back of his head. "But thanks for being so careful with my body."

I didn't want to think that this death ride was my fault so I changed the subject. "You don't still have your cell phone, do you?" I asked.

"The guy made me toss it in the dumpster," he said. And then he started wiggling.

"What's wrong?" He looked like a fish trying to get back in the bowl.

"I'm lying on something. Hold this."

I reached out a hand. "Where'd you get a flashlight?"

"Duh, I'm a Herper," he said.

I pulled my hand away.

"Herper, June," he repeated. "How do you even get by working for Dewey?"

Oh, right. Herper, as in herpetology, the study of reptiles. Not herpes, as in the big oozing cold sore disease. I wiped my hands on my jeans anyway.

He shoved the flashlight in my hand and then reached under his back and yanked my purse out into the light. It must have somehow fallen in when I was shoving him in the trunk.

"Hey, my purse."

He stuck a hand in and dug around.

"Hey, get out of my purse."

"What's this?" he asked.

I aimed the flashlight at the small bottle in his hand. How did that get in my…wait. "That girl, the one filling in for Moira at the Sheriff's office. She gave it to me."

"What girl?" Morgan asked.

I lifted up my head to get a better look at the bottle and a big fat drop of liquid rolled off my forehead and splashed on my shoulder. I pushed a hand into my tangled hair and hit the ocean. Less than five minutes in the trunk and I was already sweating like there was no tomorrow. Which there probably wasn't.

"June?" Morgan snapped his fingers near my face. "Who gave you this bottle?"

I wiped my wet hand on the carpet between us. "Some girl back at the station. Black hair with a big blue triangle." I shined the flashlight on the ceiling. Weren't car trunks suppose to have those safety thingies that you pull and the lid pops open?

Morgan gave a little whoop. "Zelda?"

"I guess." Nothing up there but rust. I waved the light over the rest of the trunk. Lots of thin, ripped carpet, a lot more rust, and one grinning idiot beside me.

"Zelda. As in Rouse. As in Rouse Blvd? As in the ever-delightful delicacy that I'm holding in my hands, *La Leche Celestial?*"

"Oh, right." They'd sponsored Metal Fest.

"And oh so wrong. What flavor is it?"

I shrugged. "Rum flavor.

He grinned. "Oh you've missed so much while you've been gone. About eight years ago, the Rouse family distillery was on the verge of bankruptcy when Grannie Rouse hit on the extremely brilliant idea of flavoring their rum with vegetables. They're so big in Japan now that they had to expand their bottling plant here in town. Pretty much everybody works there now." He gave the bottle a little shake. "And Zelda didn't say what flavor it was?"

"Who cares. Shouldn't we figure a way out of here?" I waved

the light around the trunk knowing the idea was pretty point-less. We were going to die.

He wiggled the bottle and I sighed.

"She may have said something about radishes." My last conversation on Earth was going to be with Morgan about booze.

"A prototype," he whispered as he twisted off the cap and tipped the bottle to his mouth. A small sip and he shuddered and smacked his lips.

"You gotta try it."

I hadn't eaten since, well, since my burger at Millsie's, which thanks to Morgan's house of blood, I hadn't kept in me for very long. Even a sip of alcohol was going to knock me off my ass. On the other hand, when the car stopped, we were either going to get shot or be left to dry out in the desert sun. I reached for the bottle.

My reaction was pretty similar to Morgan's. The stuff was nasty. And yet, as the fire in my throat settled, it sent a nice warm hug down to my toes.

"So why are we in a trunk?" I almost didn't want to know. Almost.

"It's a long story."

"So, just give me the gist." I poured another mouthful of radish flavored rum down my throat and shuddered in disgust.

"I gave a girl a ride."

I waited for him to go on but he seemed done. "Okay, go with the long version," I said.

He sighed and reached for the bottle. After a long sip, followed by his own shiver of disgust, he handed the bottle back to me. "You know Whiplash Ridge?"

He knew I did.

"I saw this girl hitchhiking and I gave her a ride."

"Out on Whiplash?" Serious herpers and their bored sisters trying to get out of chores were the only ones who ever went out to the Ridge. "So what happened? Was she this guy's girlfriend and you hit on her?"

"No. Well..." he shrugged his shoulders as best you can while laying flat on your back. "I might have charmed her a bit. She was hot. Hang on. Are we slowing down?"

"Quit stalling." I reached for the bottle just as the car took a sharp turn. We were thrown against the back wall of the trunk and then rolled forward as the car skidded to a halt.

Wherever we'd been headed, we'd arrived.

"Whoa." Morgan help up the half empty bottle. "I didn't spill a drop."

I could hear muffled voices outside and then a key in the lock. The trunk opened and I was blinded by sunlight. A figure reached down toward me and I did the first thing that came to mind. I kicked my boot up at the face. And missed. Somehow my laces got stuck in the locking mechanism for the trunk and I was left hanging by my foot.

Evil Looking Guy appeared and grinned down at me. "You finished?"

It looked like I was.

13

E vil Looking Guy took away my boots. Well, Dewey's boots. I never got a good look at whoever I'd tried to kick because someone slipped a pillowcase over my head. After they jammed a bandana in my mouth. They'd tried to use duct tape but I was so sweaty, it wouldn't stick.

Hands gripped my shoulders and I was shoved a few feet before I tripped over a door jam. I could hear voices but I couldn't pick out words. Somebody dropped me into a chair and I strained my ears trying to hear anything that would clue me in on what was going to happen next. There wasn't much. Lots of clicks and snapping noises. Scrapes. Something being dragged? Laughter. Close by. I didn't hear any screams of pain so Morgan was probably still alive. That was good news. Though, I wouldn't have been against a few pain-induced screams. This *was* all his fault.

I started running the past twenty-four hours over in my mind. After awhile it was hard to breathe in my hood and I think I passed out. And then somebody shook me out of my daze. I was on my feet again stumbling down a long series of uneven stone steps. By the time we'd reached the bottom, the air was cool, as if we were in a cave. I could hear voices as I was shoved along a dirt path, but I couldn't make out what anyone was saying. Was Morgan being dragged along beside me?

After what felt like forever, I heard a metallic clang. The air pressure changed and I was simultaneously assaulted with a wave of hot, dry heat and a mechanical whirring that rang in my ears. Rough hands hauled me up a set of steps and onto a smooth surface. Concrete maybe? I slid a few feet in my socks before someone kicked the back of my right leg and I dropped to my knees. And gasped. Both of my kneecaps felt like I'd collided with a brick wall. *Or the tile floor of the bathroom back at the Cactus Rose Motel. Why had I tried to catch that stupid snake?* And then the pillowcase was yanked off my head and I spit the bandana out of my mouth.

"Ow," I yelled.

"Sorry."

Evil Looking Guy leaned into view and tossed the pillowcase to a skinny Mexican guy who had a pretty big gun barrel sticking out of the waist band of his jeans.

"Compensating?" I asked. Because, you know, I'm stupid.

He grabbed his crotch. "Wanna find out, Chica?"

I really didn't. Since he seemed uninterested in following through, I decided to shut my mouth and ignore him. Hopefully, he'd return the favor.

I took a moment to look around. We were in a long, dimly lit room filled with industrial-sized washing machines that all seemed to be hard at work. The ceiling was low and covered in a patchwork of pipes held together by a lot of duct tape, spider-webs and prayers. Morgan was to my right, also on his knees, and to my left, the floor sloped to a center drain. The place was noisy, secluded and easy to clean up. All in all, it was a pretty assassination-friendly environment.

Blast.

I twisted around to see if anyone was standing behind us.

"Don't worry," a male voice shouted over the din of the

machines. I turned back around as a guy in a cheap blue suit wandered in followed by a couple more goons.

"When I have someone shot..." the rest of his words were swallowed up by one of the machines as it threw itself into some kind of spasm and began to rock violently. That threw Suit Guy into a tizzy of his own and the two new goons hustled from machine to machine, pulling plugs.

When most of the washers slowed to a stop, Suit Guy smoothed out the wrinkles in his right sleeve, adjusted the hard left part that was greased into his hair and cleared his throat. "As I was saying," he said, "when I have someone shot, I like them to see it coming, Pichoncita." The last word was drawn out. As if he knew I didn't speak Spanish. And then he winked at me.

What a douche.

"So," he said as he pointed a finger at Morgan, "are you here to return my money?"

I smacked Morgan on the arm. "You borrowed money from a gangster?" Wait. Had I just said gangster or douche? I stole a quick glance at Suit Guy. He had a grin on his face so I must not have said the D word.

"All I did was give a girl a ride," Morgan yelled.

"So why are *we* here?" I shouted back. And then it dawned on me and I turned to look at Suit Guy. "The *girl* stole money from you."

Sometimes I had moments of clarity. They never happened at the right moments of course, like when deciding whether to make a phone call or follow Morgan into a parking lot, but they did happen.

Suit Guy frowned and folded his arms over his chest. "Fifty thousand US dollars."

It wasn't an obscene amount of money but he didn't look like a real successful gangster. I smacked Morgan again. "And you didn't notice a big bag or anything?"

Suit Guy shook a finger in the air in front of me. "No, no, no.

The funds were electronically diverted from one of my business accounts."

"Oh," I said. That might not have been so noticeable.

Suit Guy gave a little nod and one of the goons hit Morgan in the back of the head. He fell flat on the floor and stayed there with his arms raised in the air.

"Hey," I yelled.

The Goon raised a hand at me, and because I'm stupid, I raised one back. Evil Looking Guy stepped closer. Maybe to protect me? There was a loud bang and we all froze as Suit Guy slammed a hand against one of the washers. He wiggled a finger at Morgan, who was still cowering flat on the floor, and Evil Looking Guy pulled him back up to his knees.

Suit Guy took a moment to adjust his tie and fiddle some more with his greasy hair before he gave Morgan his full attention. "You had a week to get me my money. Or bring me back the girl. You did neither. Tell me why I shouldn't shoot you?"

"Because your *girlfriend* actually stole the money," I said. Again. More with the stupid.

Suit Guy shifted his feet and pointed a finger at me. "Who are you?"

Blast. I really needed to learn to shut up. "I'm just an idiot who was in the wrong place at the right time." And that was the truest thing I'd ever said to anyone.

Evil Looking Guy cleared his throat. "I think she's somebody important."

Uh oh. So much for him being my protector.

That piqued Suit Guy's interest and he wandered over to me for a better look. Evil Looking Guy followed.

"I heard her yelling at him. She's mad cause she's going to have to live with her mom cause she can't cash her bonds without penalties and fees."

Suit Guy nodded in sympathy. "I hate banks." He leaned down to look at me. "They really do stick it to you with the fees, don't they?"

I felt like he was waiting for an answer but I was kinda distracted by one of the Goons who'd inched over and was making wheezing sounds as he stared down at me.

Turns out it was bothering Suit Guy too. He spun around and rattled off a few angry sounding words in Spanish. Wheezy Goon dug a cell phone from a pocket, fiddled with the screen and then shoved it in Suit Guy's face. After that, a lot more Spanish and a few confrontational chest bumps passed between them. All I caught from the conversation was *serpiente* but that was enough to tell me that I was in trouble. *Serpiente* was Spanish for snake. And that meant they'd made a connection from me to Dewey. How in the world did people keep recognizing me in these clothes? I glanced over at Morgan who was busy chewing on his right thumbnail. Well, everyone but the guy who owned the clothes.

The chat abruptly ended and Suit Guy took Wheezy Goon's cell and wandered back over to me with an amused look on his face. "June Nash, it's so nice to meet you."

"Who?" I asked. Even I thought I didn't sound very convincing.

Suit Guy crouched down in front of me and I caught sight of a tiny Rubik's Cube keychain with a half dozen keys hanging from his belt. I heard a clicking sound and looked up as he tapped the phone's screen.

It was a picture of me. Asleep on my mother's couch. In this outfit. A lot of the buttons on the checkered shirt were undone and most of the curvy silhouette on the t-shirt was visible. Under the photo, there was a caption. I squinted my eyes to read it: *June, last night, recovering from the Costa Rica trip.* Okay. That explained it. Mom had taken a photo of me while I was asleep and sent it to the guy who ran the official web page for Dewey's show, *Gone Herpin'*. It must have been her way of trying to make things appear normal. Thanks for helping, mom. I'd disown her if I thought it would stick.

"Your brother is Dewey Nash. I watch his show."

Blast. It was probably a bad thing that a gangster knew I was related to someone famous.

"*Gone Herpin'* is very good. Entertaining and informative," he continued.

Unless I could trade our freedom for a couple of autographs.

"We all watch his show." Suit Guy waved a finger at the others. Everyone but Crotch Guy nodded.

An image popped into my head of them sitting around after a hard day of torturing people and relaxing with a beer to an episode of *Gone Herpin'*. Well, all except Crotch Guy. I didn't want to think about what he did in his spare time.

I realized he was watching me watch him. "I don't think it's her," he said. "She doesn't look very important."

The small part of me holding out for the autographs in exchange for freedom scenario was tempted to argue.

"No, it's her." Wheezy Goon saved me the trouble and wiggled his fingers for the phone. When he had it back, he fiddled with the screen, waited a bit, and then waved at it. "See?"

Everyone leaned in. They stared for a long moment and then they all turned and gave me the same disappointed look that my mother had perfected when I was five.

"What?" I demanded.

"Did you really kick a fan in a wheelchair?" Suit Guy asked.

"Say what?" I tried to sound insulted but knowing me and knowing the *Dewzers*, I probably had. Those people were a crazed menace.

"Last August at a steakhouse in San Antonio," Evil Looking Guy said. He read silently over Wheezy Goon's shoulder, then clicked his tongue. "She was with her little boy."

*A lady in a wheelchair with a little boy. In San Antonio...*I flashed on a Kobe burger loaded with fresh guacamole and it came to me. *Oh yeah. Her.*

"That wasn't a wheelchair. It was one of those scooters they have in the grocery store. And she wasn't a customer at that restaurant, she'd been stalking us all day and I just wanted to eat my burger. And I didn't kick her. She rammed me when I came out of the restroom."

The looks on their faces said none of them believed me. "I did not kick her," I insisted. Then I did a half shrug. "Though, when I fell, one of my feet might have accidentally made contact with one of her knees."

"It says you kicked her multiple times," Suit Guy said.

"My foot may have bounced." More than once.

"You attacked her in front of her little boy," Wheezy Goon added.

"Hey, her little boy was nineteen and looked like he was a linebacker in his spare time." Wait. The manager had called 911 but the lady and her little darling had taken off before the police had shown up. "How do you know about that?" I asked.

"I hate June Nash dot com," Wheezy Goon said.

"Excuse me?" I put a hand on Morgan's shoulder to push myself to my feet, covered the distance in two strides and leaned over Wheezy Goon's shoulder for a look. Yep. *I hate June Nash dot com* was the title of the site all right. A sub title, under a photo of me snarling at the camera, claimed that there were over a thousand June Nash attacks to choose from.

One thousand attacks? "I have never attacked anyone in my life," I protested.

Wheezy Goon tapped at a menu button with his thumb and a list of options rolled out: *Conventions, Filming Sites, City Streets, Random* and *Submit Your Own.*

"That woman was a menace," I said. These guys obviously didn't have to deal with crazy people like the *Dewzers*. Or maybe they just shot crazy people like the *Dewzers*.

"Why are you smiling?" Wheezy Goon asked.

I swallowed the grin. "It obviously wasn't my fault because the manager of the restaurant offered to ban her for life."

"You got her banned cause she wanted an autograph?" Suit Guy asked.

"Hey, I didn't tell the guy to ban her. And she didn't want an autograph. She wanted Dewey to star in some stupid zombie movie that her kid wrote."

"That sounds kinda cool," Evil Looking Guy said.

Wheezy Goon shook his head. "Not really, there's been a lot of Zombie stuff in recent years."

They both looked over at Crotch Guy who clearly wasn't interested in the argument. He shrugged. "I guess you can't really over-saturate that genre."

"I don't know," Suit Guy joined in, "Nothing beats Romero's original. Everything nowadays is all about shocking the audience with gore."

I glanced over at Morgan who seemed just as perplexed as me by this turn in the conversation. Were we still supposed to be scared of these goons?

"I remember seeing Romero's at the midnight movies," Wheezy Goon said. "Me and my brother snuck in. That one had plenty of gore."

"In part," Suit Guy countered, "but the idea of evil lurking just inside the edge of the darkness...that's what Romero gave us and that's what all good horror should be about."

That brought Quiet Goon into the conversation. "It's not a zombie flick without gore." He growled and pantomimed a staggering zombie shoving what I guessed were brains into his open mouth.

Suit Guy wasn't having any of that and smacked his shoulder. "Wouldn't you rather be terrified by the *idea* of the zombie?"

Apparently not. Quiet Goon got in his face and the two flew into a mixture of English and Spanish. From the few words I caught, it sounded like they were arguing about the freshness of Zombies in Hollywood. Angry words soon turned to shoves and it didn't take long for the others to join in. Except for Crotch Guy. He was doing his best to separate everyone.

I backed up just in case one of them decided to make his point with a bullet.

I felt a tap on my leg and I looked down at Morgan. He was still kneeling, waiting to be told what to do. He glanced at the door across the room and then back to me. The goons were pretty occupied with the whole zombie thing but we'd have to walk right by them to get to the door.

"We'll never make it," he whispered.

He was right. We wouldn't. We needed to go on the offensive and attack them while they were distracted. I glanced around hoping for inspiration. There wasn't much. Just a lot of laundry machines. Then my eyes settled on the washer behind Morgan. It was one of the few still running. As I watched drops of water trickle down the inside of the viewing window, it kicked into a spin cycle and a shelf above it began to vibrate. A bottle of spray starch tipped over and clacked against a long brass cylinder that was topped with a dusty metal wheel and a frayed black hose. Was that an old fire extinguisher? Assuming it still worked, a dose of foamy white stuff to the eyes would buy us enough time to escape. I think I'd even seen that once in a zombie flick.

I looked over at our captors. They were still busy arguing. I let out a breath and backed up, a step at time, till I bumped against the washer. Morgan raised his shoulders in question and I ignored him. There wasn't time to explain.

I gave the goons a last glance before I hoisted myself up on the machine and grabbed at the metal ring on the fire extinguisher. It looked pretty heavy so I gave it a good yank. Turns out it was lighter than I expected. And hard to hold onto with stiff fingers. It shot out from the shelf and hurled itself over my shoulder and out of my grasp. From somewhere behind me, I heard a clang and a yelp of pain. I barely had time to wonder who'd been hit before my stocking feet slipped out from under me and my arms flew up. My fingers grasped at the air above me and latched onto a tattered strip of duct tape that dangled above my head. As I continued to fall, the pipe that it was attached to groaned in protest and there was a loud pop. That set off a chain reaction of pipes popping out of their support system and as the concrete rushed up to meet me, the ceiling rained down with a terrifying mix of steam, hot water and metal rods.

I hit the floor with a groan, rolled onto my stomach and threw my arms over my head. There was a good thirty seconds of clangs and clunks and then nothing. Somehow I'd been missed completely. I cautiously lifted my head to see how Morgan had fared.

He was still on his knee with a surprised look on his face. Like me, he'd been spared but all around him, the goons were sprawled out on the floor covered in a thick layer of pipes. The fire extinguisher lay in the middle, but I wasn't sure which idiot I'd bonked with the flying cylinder.

Wait. Where was Crotch Guy? I climbed to my feet and spun a half circle.

There he was. Behind me.

"Are you hurt?" he asked.

I was going to ask why he'd care but when I opened my mouth, my stomach had other ideas. Both men leaped out of the way as I doubled over to spit up a bunch of radish flavored liquid.

I straighten up as Crotch Guy swung an arm at my face. He was gonna hit a sick girl? What a douche. My fingers curled into a fist and I swung. He jumped back a step to avoid the punch, stumbled over a pipe and fell. *Crack.* His head hit the floor and he was down for the count.

"Hey, look," Morgan plucked a foil wrapped stick of gum out of Crotch Guy's fist.

Well, I'd totally misread that. I took the gum and popped it in my mouth. Ah, cool mint. I guess Crotch Guy wasn't such a bad guy after all.

Though, he *was* still a bad guy. And Morgan and I *had* been terrorized and held hostage. Since gum didn't make up for much, I kicked Crotch Guy in his namesake. And then stole his boat shoes.

"Let's get out of here." Morgan grabbed my hand and dragged me away.

The door we'd been brought through was locked, but the one on the other side of the laundry room led to an empty stairwell. We hustled up one flight to the lobby of a hotel well past its prime. Crotch Guy's shoes fit surprisingly well and I had no trouble keeping up with Morgan as we fell in with a parade of suits moving toward the exit. Like a flock of birds, they took an abrupt turn just before we reached freedom and swung toward the reception desk. I gripped Morgan's hand and we continued alone. We swung around a sign welcoming the *Lapel Association of North America*, slipped into a chamber of the revolving door and were spit out onto a busy sidewalk. I ran head first into a woman and my gum flew from my mouth hitting her in the shoulder. She admonished me in rapid Spanish before moving on.

Uh oh.

I did a quick spin trying to get my bearings and promptly fell against Morgan's shoulder, my head swimming in wavy images of copper cookware, brightly painted clay pots, and straw hats.

Blast.

We were in Mexico.

14

"**A**re you okay?"

"We're in Nogales," I said.

"Where'd you think we were?" Morgan asked.

I shrugged feeling a little silly. Horseshoe Bend was pretty close to Mexico and Evil Looking Guy hadn't driven us that far.

"We need to get to the border." I grabbed a handful of Morgan's shirt. Partly to steady myself, I was still feeling a little queasy, and partly because I needed to emphasize what I was about to say. "You're coming with me. Somebody official needs to see you breathing."

Morgan didn't offer any resistance which was smart on his part. Even in my state, I was confident I could kick his ass.

"You can not kick my ass," he mumbled.

Had I said that out loud? "Which way?" I asked.

There was a break in traffic. Kinda. Morgan grabbed my hand and we did the Frogger version of crossing the street, ignoring horns and dramatic arm gestures. On the other side, we ducked around a stack of rugs laid out in front of a shop, cut through a narrow alley that ran behind a pottery store and popped out onto a new street that looked pretty much like the one we'd just left. I skidded to a halt.

"What's wrong?" Morgan asked.

"Do you have any money?" Just ahead of us was a taco stand wedged in between a stall selling giant paper flowers and a pharmacy pushing little blue pills.

He shook his head. "We need to keep moving."

"I haven't eaten since yesterday." I glanced back in the direction of the hotel. There was no sign of Crotch Guy or any of the others, and the tacos smelled life saving. "If I don't get something soon, I'm gonna die." I poked a finger in Morgan's chest to emphasize each word. "Die, die, die, and die again," I said.

I was really going to die.

Morgan knocked my finger away. "Same thing's gonna happen if those guys catch up to us."

"Well, I want a taco." I dragged Morgan over to the stand. "How much?" I asked the guy. This close to the border, chances were really good that he spoke better English than me.

Taco Guy replied with a bunch of Spanish. Thanks to the translators that Dewey's network always provide on our travels, I have a very limited knowledge of the languages I'm exposed to. When I'm on my own, pretty much all I can do is ask for directions to the bathroom or curse like a land-locked sailor. Since none of the words that Taco Guy used had anything to do with my two areas of expertise I turned to Morgan for help.

"That guy took my wallet back at the Strand," he said. Just to prove it, he dug through all the pockets of his cargo shorts and produced two quarters, three dimes and a rubber band.

"I really need food." I knew I was whining but there was nothing I could do about that. And then inspiration struck. "Hey, you got anything we could trade with him?"

Morgan shook his head and casually slipped his right hand over his watch.

"One taco. One kiss." Taco Guy offered. Turns out he knew more English than he let on.

One taco, one kiss. It didn't sound like that bad a deal.

"You'd kiss a stranger for a taco?" Morgan asked. For some reason, he made it sound like it *was* a bad deal.

"Maybe."

The tacos smelled delicious and my mouth was minty fresh thanks to Crotch Guy's gum.

Morgan held up a finger and mumbled something in Spanish to Taco Guy. Then he dragged me a few feet away. "The border's just up this street and one over."

"I want a taco." I was digging in my heels.

"Fine. I'm gonna go make sure the coast is clear. Do what you have to and we'll meet back up at the end of the street." And then he took off. Part of me wanted to race after him, I didn't like the idea of letting him out of my sight, but most of me wanted food. I moved a step closer to the stand and Taco Guy grinned at me.

∾

y the time we'd reconnected, halfway up the block, I'd eaten three of my five tacos.

Morgan eyed me as I offered him the last two. I really didn't want to share but I kinda felt like it was the decent thing to do.

"Did you..." he looked like he really didn't want to know.

I shook my head. "Turns out he's a Gone Herpin' fan."

I didn't want to admit to Morgan how close I'd come to puckering up before I'd spotted the Gone Herpin' sticker on the ground beef container. "I told the guy that Dewey would take him on a personal tour of the studio the next time he's in Horseshoe Bend."

"Dewey doesn't have a studio," Morgan said. "Everything's shot out in the field."

"He doesn't know that." All was fair with reptiles and tacos. Or something like that. I'd be smartish again once the food hit my brain.

"You shouldn't have told him who you were," Morgan said.

"Who is he gonna tell? It's not like the bad guys are gonna stop at the taco stand to see if we happened by." To make my point I turned and gestured down the block. At that moment, the crowds on the sidewalk cleared enough to give us a good view of the stand and for some reason, Taco Guy was pointing right back at me. Why would he...? Wait...was that Crotch Guy standing beside him?

Blast. I hated being wrong.

"This way." Morgan threw the tacos in a nearby trash can then grabbed my hand and dragged me away before I could dig them back out.

15

We lost Crotch Guy somewhere between a rug shop and a dental office. I'd waved to a confused hygienist as Morgan had asked about a back door. We plowed through their alley, took a couple of turns, and then popped out across the street from the covered walkway that led to the US-Mexico border.

On any given day, the crowds going home are pretty thin and it takes about five minutes to get through the line. Today, we weren't going to be so lucky. A thick cluster of senior citizens snaked up the sidewalk in front of us. From the looks of things, they'd been on a discount-drug-buying tour. Pretty much any prescription you needed could be found south of the border at a drastically reduced price, and these folks had had a good time. Multiple bags with pharmacy logos dangled from every liver-spotted hand.

I did a quick tally and lost count at thirty. Most of the seniors had canes but there were a few walkers sprinkled into the mix. Directly in front of us, a really old guy with a fancy waxed mustache was propped up against a lady in her forties. He looked like he was beyond the help of whatever was in his bags.

This was going to take a while.

I gave Morgan a sideways glance. He was busy keeping an eye on the street behind us and didn't notice me looking him over. This was the first quiet moment we'd had since he'd reappeared in my life and I forced myself to think about the last time I'd seen him. It had been two days after high school graduation and three days before Dewey and I left for our graduation trip to Egypt.

That hadn't been my first choice, of course. Or Dewey's. I'd wanted St. Thomas and he'd pushed for Costa Rica. Egypt had come about because of the turn of a page.

Mom had been after me to make a decision about what I wanted to study in college. Scrunching up my serious face and telling her I was still deciding only worked for so long. One night she'd finally had enough. She'd blocked my view of the TV and said, "June you need to make a decision. You graduate high school in six months. Be an adult like your brother. He knows exactly what he's going to do with his life."

Of course he did. He'd known he'd wanted to work with creepy crawlies since he'd found that first snake in our backyard minutes after moving to Horseshoe Bend when we were five. I wasn't so lucky. Even now at twenty-seven I was still clueless. Thankfully, I still had time. I wouldn't have to worry about a career of my own until Dewey was done being famous.

"So, what's your plan June?" Mom had said. "I'm not sending you to college just to party."

Shoot. That had been my plan. To get her off my back once and for all, I picked up one of the college catalogs that she'd left scattered all over the house, flipped it open and pointed to a random photo. Thanks to the design layout of a graphic artist I'll never meet, I ended up going to school to study Archeology. Hence the trip to Egypt. In the end, my random choice had turned out okay because Archeology students really knew how to dig up a party.

"What's so funny?" Morgan asked.

"Huh?" I glanced around. Was the crowd starting to move?

"You were laughing."

Was I?

I shrugged and watched a geezer try to get his walker, oxygen tank and half a dozen shopping bags through a turnstiles at the front of the covered walkway without dropping anything or accepting a lick of help. When the old guy'd made it through, Morgan turned his attention back to the street and I tried to remember what I'd just been thinking about.

Up ahead of us a lady started taking selfies with what I guessed where her favorite purchases of the day. I leaned forward and tapped her arm. "Can you call the states on that?" I asked.

Though we were practically on top of the border that separated the U.S. from Mexico, if you didn't have the right calling plan, your cell wasn't good for much more than what she was currently doing with it.

The lady responded by tucking her phone into the zippered portion of her purse and jamming a flowery hat on her head that blocked my view of pretty much the entire world. I glanced around at the people that I could still see and everybody within earshot gave me a *don't ask me either* look and moved as far as way as the line would permit.

Morgan bumped my shoulder with his. "I'm really sorry about getting you kidnapped."

"Why didn't you just go to Warren?" I asked.

He went back to scanning the crowd. "What?"

"When the douche back there came after you for the fifty grand. Why didn't you call Warren? He would've helped you."

"I didn't want to go to him empty handed."

I frowned. "Is that why you were at The Strand?" I asked. "Where you looking for that girl and the fifty grand?"

"Something like that."

"You should have just told Warren what was going on," I said.

Morgan wiggled his mouth a bit, like he was thinking about it. "The guy made threats."

"All the more reason to go to Warren," I insisted.

"He didn't threaten me." Morgan tightened his jaw and I felt my heart break a little.

"Cyrano," I whispered.

And then I slapped my forehead. Oh blast, the hound! Once again, I'd forgotten all about her. "We left without Cyrano." I twisted around as if I expected to see her in the crowd behind us.

"He gave her to some guy." Morgan sniffed and scratched at his left eye.

"What guy?" I asked. My fingers wanted to form a fist but my hand was still throbbing from all the punching I'd done in the last twelve hours.

Morgan shrugged. "I watched them put her in a car and it drove away."

"Wait, you weren't blindfolded?" My eyes had been covered as soon as they'd unhooked my foot from Evil Looking Guy's trunk.

Morgan scratched at his eyes again. "She's long gone."

I slipped a hand through the crook of his arm. "Look, we'll get up to the guard, we'll get them to call Warren, he'll put out one of those bulletin thingies and you'll have her back in no time."

"Maybe."

I pulled him closer and squeezed. "Hey," I said. "You're kind of a hero."

Morgan shot me a sideways glance. "How do you figure that?"

"You faked your death to save your dog. There's something very noble about that." I said. And very stupid, because it was a lousy long-term solution. And Dewey had ended up in jail because of it. Still. You had to admire the gesture.

Blast. Now my ten-year-old grudge with him seemed a little silly. "I forgive you," I said.

"Thanks." Morgan stood on his tip toes, trying to see around the hat in front of us. "I really do feel bad that you got dragged into this."

"No," I said. "I forgive you for the thing with the rattlesnakes."

He turned to look at me. "What rattlesnakes?"

Despite the pain, my fingers curled back into that comfortable fist. "What do you mean, what rattlesnakes?"

He shrugged.

"Two days before graduation," I said. "Dewey's demonstration? The rattlesnakes?"

Morgan just stared at me blankly.

"The public access station thing? You talked me into helping out and then you didn't tell me that Dewey was going to...." I tried to shiver the thought away. "Sex the snake," I whispered.

Morgan's face softened and he grinned. He actually grinned. "Is that why you're mad at me? Cause Dewey popped a snake and you didn't look away in time."

"Hey, it's gross."

"It's really not."

"Stuff pokes out."

"The hemipenes. If it's a male," he added.

"Whatever." I poked a finger into his chest. "I fainted and hit my head and bled everywhere. You made me look like a fool on national TV."

"Public access." He laughed. "Nobody saw it."

"That show won some stupid national award."

"For public access."

This was not how I'd spent the last ten years picturing this conversation. In the hundreds of times it had played out in my mind, most had ended with me resting a foot on Morgan's broken lifeless body. While he cried.

"And it wasn't rattlesnakes, plural," he said. "It was rattlesnake, one."

"No," I said. "I close my eyes and I distinctly see three, no four stacks of cages."

"Yeah, they were empty. It was for show. We borrowed them from Lon's Pet Supply."

"We did?"

"We did. You drove."

"I have absolutely no memory of..." *Wait.* "What do you mean by, *is that why you're mad at me?*"

"Huh?" Morgan developed a sudden interest in the crowd.

"Is there another reason I should be mad at you?" I asked

"We've got a problem," he said.

"We do if you did something else to me," I told him.

"No." Morgan pulled me to one side of the flowery hat. About twenty feet ahead of us, a uniformed Mexican cop was talking with somebody I couldn't see, thanks to the crowd. I leaned a bit more and as everyone shifted, a face came into view.

Blast. The somebody was Crotch Guy.

Lately, my luck just sucked.

nd then it got worse. Crotch Guy unfolded an 8x10 and passed it to the cop. I only got a quick glance but even from this distance I recognized my hair. It was the same photo that Ticket Girl had shown me back at the snake show. Blast. Everybody had that photo but me.

Morgan pulled us back behind the flower-covered hat. "We need to get out of here."

"Do you think the cop's dirty?" I asked. "Maybe Crotch Guy's just trying to fool him into catching us."

Morgan's eye widened a bit. "Crotch Guy?"

"He didn't introduce himself." I jerked a thumb at the fence. "We're so close." We were just steps away from saving Dewey. If we shoved all the old people aside. "Can't we just make a run for it. Tell the American border side who we are."

"I don't think we can get past that cop, and the American guards can't cross into Mexico."

"But they could call Warren," I said.

"And if the cop *is* dirty, we'll be dead by the time he gets the message. We need to lay low and try to cross later."

"Fine." I let Morgan take my hand.

As we slipped through the crowd, I glanced back in time to

see Crotch Guy cup his goodies for a moment before shaking it off. I couldn't help but smile. That'll teach you, I thought.

~

M organ skidded to a halt when we'd reached the other side of town.

"Why are we stopping?" I turned and followed his gaze. Directly across the street from us, there was a coffee shop with a bank of computers visible through the plate glass window. Even from here I could make out the sign with the international symbol for the Internet.

"You're a genius." We could email for help.

Morgan's face lit up with a lopsided grin and a butterfly in my stomach did a tiny somersault.

What the...*oh this was not good*. I did not want to think about Morgan that way. He was my brother's best friend, a snake nut, *and* he'd made a fool out of me on television. Well, it had only been public access, but still. My demise had been viewed by at least a dozen people.

I glanced back at the cafe as a twenty-something girl in a yellow sundress dropped into a chair at the window and raised a giant cinnamon roll to her lips. The acrobatic butterfly in my tummy returned and did what probably amounted to an Olympic level floor routine. Oh, thank God. I wasn't in love. I was just hungry.

"What?" Morgan gave me a quizzical look.

I shrugged. Telling someone that you were glad that you weren't in love with them seemed rather rude. Even for me. "Nothing," I said. "It just looks good."

Morgan nodded. "She sure does."

I ignored the comment. "We still have a problem though," I reminded him. "We don't have any money and the chances are pretty good that you have to pay to use the computers." If they worked like the ones in the States, you'd get a password only after you'd bought at least a cup of coffee.

Morgan shook his head. "We don't need any money," he said. "All we need is for *her* to send a message for *us*."

We both turned to watch Cinnamon Roll Girl wipe her fingers on a napkin and then attack the keyboard of her laptop.

"That is an excellent idea," I said.

Morgan did the lopsided grin again, my butterfly danced some more and I groaned and grabbed his hand. "Come on."

Up ahead, the traffic signal turned red and we darted out in front of a bright yellow sports car that was still deciding if it was going to stop for the light. The driver slammed on his brakes setting off a chain reaction of squeals. Horns honked and everyone made sure we got their own specific take on the obscene gesture of the day as we hustled across the road and through the open door of the cafe.

The place was dead. There was a short line at the pastry counter but Cinnamon Roll Girl was the only one at a table. The bank of computers along the far wall weren't even turned on.

Morgan dragged us away from the front window and we slipped behind a display table full of coffee related souvenirs. He took a long moment to check out Cinnamon Roll Girl, and I wondered how many tourists went home with an *I got beaned at Nellies in Nogales* travel mug.

"What's Warren's email?" Morgan asked.

"I don't know." I shrugged as an old lady in a white starch apron strolled by with a tray of the flakiest looking fruit filled pastries that I'd ever seen in my life. She set them on a platter in the display case and I licked my lips thinking about what eighty American cents might buy. Probably half a strawberry.

"June?" Morgan bumped my shoulder.

I shrugged. "I just start typing someone's name and my computer fills in the rest."

"What do you want me to do?" he asked.

"Can't you just Google the Sheriff's department in Horseshoe Bend?" I didn't know why he was making this so difficult.

"Because nothing on that page is going to be for emergencies and we need to get in touch with someone right now. Does your mom have an email?" Morgan asked.

"She does," I said.

"Do you remember it?"

"I don't," I admitted. But that wasn't my fault. Her email address was some sort of play on a weird phrase that had something to do with a character from one of her favorite TV shows. I got a headache just thinking about it.

"Do you know anybody else?" Morgan asked.

Was that supposed to be some sort of comment on my social life? "How about we email somebody *you* know?"

He gave me a sheepish look and shrugged. "Auto fill-in." Then he brightened. "How about Dewey? They're probably monitoring his email."

"Do you know it?"

"You don't?" he asked.

"We text. Or I shout across the room. Look, just go over there and send one to Dewey and one to the Sheriff's page."

Morgan took a half a step and then turned back.

"You know, Whiplash Ridge isn't too far from here. I'm pretty sure that once we jumped the fence, a border patrol helicopter would spot us and send someone to investigate. I doubt we'd have to hike very far."

There was no way I was doing that. "What's the matter? You afraid you won't be able to charm that girl into letting you use her computer?"

He took the bait and stepped out from behind souvenir mugs. Cinnamon Roll Girl looked up and Morgan bobbed his head at her. After a moment, she returned his smile. Then her eyes settled on me and she frowned.

"Go away," Morgan said out of the corner of his mouth.

"Give me your change." I was going to get a cup of coffee. And I wasn't going to share.

Once the coins were jingling in my hand, I fell into line at the pastry case. There were only three other customers but I had a feeling that this was going to take just shy of forever. The lady at the front was having a hard time deciding what she wanted and from all the hand gestures that she and the cashier were throwing at each other, it looked like she wasn't interested in stepping to one side while she tried to figure it out. I leaned against a table for two and kept an eye on the front window. Just in case Suit Guy or his friends happened by. For the moment, I was partially blocked by the souvenir display but when the line started to shrink I was going to be exposed. The sooner the email was sent, the better. I glanced over at Cinnamon Roll Girl's table. Morgan was sitting across from her. At least she hadn't told him to scram. Yet.

The old lady in the white starch apron had ditched the pastry tray and was now on cleanup duty. She caught my eye, smiled as she slapped a wet rag on a table and then headed for the trash can. She got a half dozen steps before she did an about face.

"No!"

Uh oh. I looked around hoping she wasn't talking to me. Of course she was.

"No, no, no, no." her voice got louder as she got closer and when she was about a foot away, she started ranting in Spanish. All I caught was *Serpiente.* Blast. Another angry Dewzer. I had to get out of these clothes.

I looked around for Morgan but he was deep in conversation with Cinnamon Roll Girl and neither one was looking at her computer. Or in my direction. How could they seriously not hear this woman's freakout?

I waved my arms trying to get his attention. The old lady stepped into my line of sight and snapped the rag, hitting me in the hand.

"Ow," I yelped.

She rattled off some more words that sounded very much like a threat and the customer in front of me tapped my arm. "She said you have to leave or she'll burn down the place with you in it."

Well, at least I'd gotten the tone right. "Morgan," I yelled.

He appeared and I danced around the snapping towel to hide behind his back.

"What did you do?" he asked as Rag Lady continued her tirade.

"Nothing," I insisted. "Did you send the message?"

"You'd better." Morgan raised a hand and began to charm Rag Lady with a bunch of soothing Spanish.

Over at the window, Cinnamon Girl had left her computer unattended and was standing a couple of feet to one side, completely riveted by Rag Lady's drama. Everybody in the place was. I glanced over at Morgan. He'd gotten the woman into a seat at a corner table and was kneeling down beside her while she waved her arms about and spewed lots of nasty sounding words.

While he kept her busy, I slid into Cinnamon Roll Girl's chair and considered her computer screen. Her email was up! One hurdle down. I closed the message she'd been writing and clicked for a new one. When the email box opened, I poised my fingers over the keyboard. Who was I going to send this to? I glanced back at Morgan. He was doing a pretty good job of calming down Rag Lady. Her hands were in her lap now, so I knew I had a few minutes before she looked this way and remembered that she hated me.

I couldn't blame her though. Right now, *I* hated me. I sighed and picked at Cinnamon Roll Girl's cinnamon roll. If I hadn't been so bent up on avoiding *Dewzers*, I'd have realized that Morgan was Morgan a lot sooner than I did. And if I'd just made that call to Warren, back at The Strand, I wouldn't be stuck in Mexico hiding from a bunch of idiot gangsters. I'd had so many chances to save Dewey and I'd made a complete mess out of all of them.

Maybe I did need a break from this job. For Dewey's sake. But what would I do instead? Archaeology? I'd never even taken my degree out for a test drive. *And* I'd graduated ages ago. Well, not ages. It had only been four, no five years. Old stuff *was* still going to be old stuff. Maybe if I found someone I trusted enough to fill in for me with Dewey, I could ditch the snake world for a while and try digging around in remote piles of...wait...snakes.

Ingrid the snake charmer at gmail dot com popped into my head. I typed it in the email's address box and then quickly deleted it. No. I couldn't contact Alvaro's granddaughter. I was pretty sure I'd never sent her that last 8x10 glossy of Dewey. Besides, she was thirteen. And a *Dewzer.* They were nuts. Especially when someone came between them and their...wait....Sammy at hah dot com. I could email the president of the Herpetology Association of Horseshoe Bend. He was an adult. Sort of. He could contact Warren. My fingers flew over the keys.

Sammy,

This is June Nash. Emergency. Call Sheriff Mitchell and tell him Morgan is with me and ask if he'll meet us up on Whiplash Ridge. We need a ride home. Thanks.

June

Sorry about puking on you back in high school.

That last line seemed important, in case he was one of the H.A.H. people I'd barfed on all those years ago.

I hit send and stuffed the last chunk of the cinnamon roll in my mouth. I caught Morgan's eye and slipped out the door with a couple of other people who'd gotten bored now that Rag Lady had calmed down. My savior caught up with me around the corner and we didn't stop running till we'd cut through a couple of alleys and stumbled out onto a small residential side street.

"What was that all about?" I asked when we stopped to catch our breath.

"Uhh," he closed his eyes, "she said you were the devil incarnate and you made her cry when you wouldn't let her take a picture with that sexy snake man."

I sighed. Another entry for *I Hate June Nash dot com*. "That's all she said?" I asked, "because she was pretty chatty."

"She did say a lot of things about you personally," Morgan said. "I think she might have invoked some voodoo."

I couldn't tell if he was being serious. "Voodoo is Haiti not Mexico."

"I'm pretty sure I heard a voodoo curse. See, this is why that website exists. The Dewzers don't like you keeping them away from their man."

"Forget about the voodoo," I said. "It's like five thousand degrees out here. There's no way we can hike up The Ridge in this heat."

"You sent the message?"

"Yeah."

"Okay." Morgan led me over to a trashcan with about a half dozen partially filled water bottles in view.

I shook my head. "I'm not drinking someone's leftovers."

"We'll wash them out and refill them at the gas station. Or we can stand here until one of those guys from the laundry tracks us down." He grabbed two bottles off the top and tried to hand me one.

I waved it away. "I wanna pick out my own and wash it myself."

"Hurry," he said. He headed for the shadows of what looked like an apartment building.

I did a quick eeny meany with the rest of the bottles, grabbed the winner and then used a chunk of my shirt to twist off the cap. At the curb I emptied the left over water onto the street, careful not to splash any on my pants. Who knew what diseases its previous owner had. As I shook out the last drops, I wandered over to the apartment building to join Morgan. The shadows were empty. Where'd he go? The sidewalk was deserted and there were only a few cars in the distance. I did a quick spin and spotted a narrow alley next to the apartment building. Morgan *had* said we needed to get out of sight. I scrambled over and took the corner as Crotch Guy emerged from the alley. He didn't look surprised to see me.

"We must be quick," he said.

I screamed and bonked him on the forehead with my water bottle. And then I screamed again and brought the heel of the boat shoe I'd stolen from him down hard on his bare foot. He squealed and went down in a jumbled mess.

Halfway up the alley, Morgan peeked out from behind a row of dumpsters, his mouth open in surprise.

"Run!" I screamed.

I darted out of the alley and ran straight into Wheezy Goon's arms. He was covered in cuts and bruises and a lot of bandages tinted in red. The pipes from the ceiling had really done a number on him. I twisted and kicked until he grabbed a handful of my hair close to the scalp and held me just of range.

"Ow," I cried trying to peel his fingers free.

"Hold still then," he said.

Had Morgan gotten away? "Call Warren," I yelled at the sky. Just in case.

Wheezy Goon let go of my hair and slapped my face hard enough to snap my head back. The world did a few spins and I had a hard time keeping my eyes from rolling around in my head.

I think I was picked up. I seemed to float over to a van. A door slid open and Wheezy Goon tossed me in on the seatless floor. I struggled to sit up and then leaned against a wall and touched my face. My cheek burned and my nose felt like I'd been hit with a can of beans. It had to be broken. No blood on my fingers though. Wait. I hadn't heard any crunching. Dewey had broken his nose once and I remember him telling me how he heard everything crunch when my fist had made contact.

A banged-up-looking Quiet Goon appeared in the door, carrying Crotch Guy who was breathing funny. The toes on the foot I'd stomped were all pointing in different directions. Good. Served him right for hanging around with the wrong crowd. As a hood was thrown over my head, I caught Crotch Guy's eye and for a moment, just a moment, he looked disappointed. Why would he look...*wait*...had he said *we* back there in the alley? Why would he say *we*? Unless...had he been trying to help? *We must be quick* kinda seemed like something you'd say if you were trying to help someone. He *had* offered me gum back in the laundry. Before I'd rearranged his boys.

Blast.

I'd misread the situation.

Again.

17

When Evil Looking Guy took the hood off this time, I was perched on the edge of a hotel bed. I'd fully expected to end up back by the drain in the laundry so this was a pleasant surprise. Well, except for the tape around my wrists and ankles. And the strip over my mouth. Wheezy Goon had decided I'd been too chatty back in the van. I'd only asked one question. If he and Quiet Goon had planned on being roommates in prison.

I realized Evil Looking Guy was hovering and I looked up at him. Blast. He was covered in as many bandages as his friends had been. And something about his face said we had unfinished business. I turned away.

The place we were in had that *I used to be fancy back in the day* feel to it. Lots of wrought iron and marbled features. The flowered wallpaper was faded and peeling away at the ceiling but the mattress under the lacy spread was comfortable.

No sign of any of the other goons. Or Morgan. Maybe he'd made it to the border wall. No sign of Crotch Guy either. Would they take him to the hospital? If he really was a cop, he could call Warren and tell him…what would he tell him? Would he know where they'd taken me? Maybe.

Blast.

"Welcome back, Pichoncita."

I twisted around. Suit Guy was watching me from a chair at the desk, a shiny, silver handgun in his lap. He looked just as bad as the others. Behind him, a wall of heavy red curtains hung from a fancy rod with curlycue ends. Mom would love this place. I wondered if she and Warren had done the romantic weekend thing yet. Then I shivered and tried not to think about the possibility that Mom and Warren had done the romantic weekend thing yet.

Suit Guy waved the gun at Evil Looking Guy. "Sit down."

I got one more angry look and the goon wandered over to an empty chair near the door and started fiddling with his cell phone.

"Nice place, huh?"

I turned back to Suit Guy. I couldn't say anything because of the duct tape, so I just nodded.

"Built in 1922," he went on. "She's still a nice hotel, isn't she." He pantomimed pulling something off his lips and then pointed a finger at my lap.

I lifted my bound hands to my mouth and he nodded so I tugged at the tape until it ripped free, taking a layer of skin with it. Blast. I wiggled my face trying to get the feeling back into what was left of my lips.

"Comfy?" he asked.

"I am, thanks," I had a bad feeling that it wasn't going to last. For now, I needed to keep things pleasant, and hope that Morgan had somehow gotten in touch with Warren.

Suit Guy tucked his gun into a shoulder holster and brought a leather binder over for me to read. It was a menu.

"Hungry? I know I am," he said. "It's been such a crazy day, I haven't had a chance to eat anything since breakfast."

He was much calmer than I'd have expected. Considering I'd almost killed him by pipe. Even if that hadn't been my original intention.

"See anything you like?" he asked. He gave me a moment and turned a page.

I was a little too freaked out to really focus on the words in front of me but there was no way I was going to let him know that. "I'll take fajitas." I had no idea if they were on the menu but seeing as how this was a touristy part of Mexico, I felt like it was a pretty safe bet.

Suit Guy smiled. Did he realize how scared I was? Probably.

"Chicken or steak?"

"Chicken," I said. It didn't really matter. My stomach was growling and I was a nervous eater. Given the opportunity, I was going to scarf down whatever was put in front of my face while I waited for them to eventually shoot me.

"Wonderful, we'll all have the same thing."

He tossed the menu on the desk and I caught sight of a digital clock. 3:57. Blast. I had less than twenty-four hours to find Morgan, stick him in Warren's line of sight and deliver Dewey to the Strand in time for his lecture. Of course, all that hinged on me getting out of this hotel room without getting shot. Considering the tape around my hands and feet, and Suit Guy's big silver gun, I wasn't real confident about my chances. If I died, I was haunting Morgan for the rest of his pathetic life.

Suit Guy snapped his fingers and Evil Looking Guy jumped up.

"Wait while they fix the food. I want everything piping hot." He looked over at me and offered an apologetic look. "Grand as she is, the room service is not what it used to be."

Evil Looking Guy pocketed his cell and hurried off. I tried not to look too interested in the desk phone that was now half hidden by the menu.

"So, Pichoncita," Suit Guy said, "you ran off so quickly, we didn't get to finish our business downstairs."

"Morgan didn't take your money," I may have peppered that with some of my favorite words. So much for pleasant. I seemed to be stuck in *annoy the guy who wants to kill you* mode.

"You ever own a home?"

That was an unexpected comeback. I shook my head.

"I've owned several," he said.

He didn't look the type but since I really needed to start keeping my mouth shut, I sucked in my top lip and waited.

"Sometimes, you buy a house, you get a really great mortgage rate and you love the company you're with. If you have a question, someone is always at the other end of the phone and you actually enjoy mailing these people your monthly payment. And then, suddenly, without warning, they go and sell your mortgage to someone else. You complain of course but they only shrug. You're not their problem anymore. Well. That's our relationship now. I've sold the debt to a business associate." He made a point to glance at his watch. "Tabor and Nesto should be picking him up from the airport right about now."

Probably the two missing goons.

"When they get back, you can discuss your concerns with him."

"I'm not giving anybody fifty thousand...."

Suit Guy wagged a finger at me and I sucked my top lip back in.

"You misunderstand," he said. "Tegu's not coming here to collect money. He's coming here to collect you."

I forgot I was tied up and tried to stand. And tipped over. "You sold me?" I yelled as I wiggled myself upright. "You can't sell people." That wasn't something that happened in real life. Was it?

"Turns out, Tegu is a fan."

Great. Another *Dewzer*. However...."So he likes my brother's show?" The freedom for autographs thing popped back into my head. Or maybe a studio tour like I'd promised Taco Guy. Either idea might work.

"You misunderstand. Tegu's a fan of *yours*."

Uh oh. Neither idea was gonna work. I had a feeling, Tegu was going to want more than what I was willing to offer.

"He's on his way, but we have plenty of time to eat before he gets here. In the meantime," Suit Guy stood and tugged open the drapes, "let's just sit quietly and enjoy the view while we wait for our food." He flipped the desk chair to face the window and unclipped the tiny Rubik's Cube keychain from his belt.

While he worked the puzzle, I gave the room a good once-over. Two beds, an empty coffee maker, and an open door that probably led to the bathroom. I didn't see anything laying around that I could use as a weapon and with my ankles taped together, there was no way I could beat Suit Guy to the door. Or even the phone on the desk three feet away. I'd not only have to hope that the operator answered on the first ring but that the word *help* was universal. For the moment, I was stuck. I cursed Morgan to a slow agonizing death, after Warren laid eyeballs on him, of course, and I shifted until I could see out the window too.

We were up high. I couldn't see the street from my spot on the bed, so I figured we had to be on the fourth or fifth floor. Off in the distance, a few puffy white clouds dotted the light blue sky. Not enough to cool down the day, but enough to lull you into a false sense of security. The heat would have been deadly if we'd have made it out to Whiplash Ridge. Was Warren out there right now looking for me? Had Sammy even gotten the email I'd sent from the cafe? And what about this Tegu guy? What was he gonna want? Well, I had a feeling I knew what he was gonna want. And he was going to be sadly disappointed. I'm a biter. And on the back end of thirty-six bad hours.

Before I could work myself into any more of a tizzy, the room door popped open and a heavenly smell almost knocked me off the bed.

"Finally," Suit Guy said. He got up and clipped the Rubik's Cube back on to his belt. The food hadn't taken that long but I got the feeling that the guy liked stepping on his goons whenever he got the chance.

Evil Looking Guy set the rickety cart in front of me and

jabbed a finger at a little metal can nestled in a rack under the chaffing dish. "I had to wait while they found a warmer thingy, okay?"

Beer, plates, napkins, lots of silverware and a couple of oven mitts rounded out the rest of the table.

Suit Guy strolled over and took all the utensils just as I was deciding which knife would look best sticking out of his chest.

"Don't worry," he told me. "Fajitas are finger food."

Blast.

He dumped everything by the phone and then he and Evil Looking Guy did an awkward dance as each tried to get around the other in the narrow space by the desk. Suit Guy finally smacked his lackey a few times. "What are you doing?"

"I need my charger," Evil Looking Guy pointed down at a gym bag on the floor behind Suit Guy. "I'm down to six percent."

"Then stop playing games on it." Suit Guy gave him a couple more smacks before he let him through. Evil Looking Guy dropped to a knee and started digging through his bag. After a quick adjustment to his greasy hair Suit Guy wandered back over to me and used one of the oven mitts to lift the lid off the chaffing dish. "Be careful," he said. "This stuff is sizzling."

And it was. Strips of chicken and peppers were dancing around in a bubbling sauce. As he dropped the mitt back on the table, an inkling of an idea tickled my brain. Then I realized that Suit Guy was hovering.

I looked up as he leaned in close and ran the back of a finger along my throat. "Maybe I shouldn't have made that deal with Tegu, Pichoncita." And then his hand worked its way through my hair and he stroked my earlobe. I shivered and flashed on the bane of my childhood. The wet willy.

As kids, Dewey loved to torment me by licking his fingers and sticking them in my ears. I'd retaliate by twisting his nipples. Chaos would ensue. He'd scream, I'd shriek, and mom would lock us in the pantry till we calmed down. Or she needed snacks.

So when Suit Guy's finger slipped into my ear, a shudder ran from my lobe to the base of my spine and I was seven years old again. My reflexes kicked in and I swung my hands up to block him. Since my wrists were bound together, I had the combined force of two arms and a lot of pent up anger. My thumbs caught Suit Guy in the throat. He dropped to the carpet beside me and got out a single gurgle before my knees snapped his mouth shut. His eyes glazed over and he rolled onto his back like the roach he was.

I raised my hands over my head and brought them down hard on my thighs. The tape split and my hands were free. *Thank you mostly time-sucking YouTube videos.* Then I leaned over and twisted Suit Guy's nipples through his shirt. If nothing else, I'm a girl who likes closure.

Over at the wall outlet, Evil Looking Guy was about to plug in the power cord for his phone charger. As he turned to see what the commotion was, the grease that was sizzling the fajitas popped. I looked down at the chaffing dish and the inkling from earlier became a full-fledged idea.

I threw my hands into the oven mitts, grabbed the chaffing dish by the handles, and chucked lunch at Evil Looking Guy's head. And missed. Everything crashed into the window and the little metal warming can dropped into the gym bag. There was a moment of silence then the bag burst in flames. A hot second later, the curtains were goners.

Evil Looking Guy let out a high-pitched scream and knocked me over on his way out. I crawled across Suit Guy and hauled myself up by the edge of the desk. Overhead, black smoke was pouring out of flames that were doing a pretty good job of devouring the curtains. I grabbed a knife that was just shy of scalding and dropped to the floor to roll away from the heat.

By the time I'd sliced through the tape around my ankles, the lamp on the desk had burst into flames, taking the phone with it. I decided to call Warren from the lobby.

I leaped over Suit Guy and was almost to the door before I skidded to a halt. I couldn't leave him. Even if he deserved it. I went back and grabbed his ankles. I expected him to weigh a ton but I was across the room before I realized it. Fire was certainly motivating. At the door, I turned the knob and then bounced it open with my butt. Once I had him in the hall, I dropped his legs and sucked in a lungful of stale hotel air.

"Fire!" I screamed.

Nothing happened. Except for Suit Guy making some groany noises and rolling his head from side to side.

I glanced up and down the empty hall. We were only a few doors down from the elevator. And right next to the call buttons was a lovely little fire alarm box. I dashed down there and gave the handle a yank. From somewhere deep in the hotel, an alarm began to clang.

Moments later, people spilled out of the rooms. Weird thing though, I'd been expecting vacationing families. You know, mom, dad, kids, maybe a grandma or two. Instead, the crowd consisted of men and women in various stages of undress: lacy garments, tighty-whities, black socks and a suit vest or jacket here and there. A guy in a red teddy with a riding crop skirted around me and I was almost knocked over by a woman who was naked except for the feathers dangling from her pierced nipples. *Oh yeah.* The convention! No wonder no one noticed me being brought in with a hood over my head.

As I fought my way to the stairs, I thought I heard my name. Had Suit Guy come to? I spun around to look, but before I could get a fix on any of the faces, I was swept with the crowd into the stairwell. Three flights down, I spilled out into the lobby with the rest of the group.

Across the way at the revolving door, I could see Wheezy Goon and Quiet Goon trying to fight their way into the hotel through the escaping crowd. Now what? The back door? Maybe a way out through the kitchen? Or maybe...*a secret door....*

"June!"

I got through most of a 360 before I caught sight of Morgan near the elevators.

"Stay there," he yelled.

Like I was going anywhere else? I pressed myself against the wall and watched him push his way through the fleeing bodies. Just how many people were staying in this place? Behind him, the elevator doors slid open and another wave poured out. The momentum shoved Morgan through the crowd and he was thrown into the wall beside me.

"Where have you been?" I shouted.

"Upstairs," he shouted back. He was right in front of me and I could barely hear him. "I was going to rescue you."

The voice I'd heard in the hall. I pulled him close so I could yell in his ear. "I don't need rescuing."

He twisted me so he could scream in *my* ear. "Obviously. I don't even want to know what you did to Neymar."

"Who?"

"The guy with the greasy hair."

Oh. *Suit Guy.* "You left me in that stupid alley, Morgan."

"And you'd be home by now if you hadn't attacked that cop."

I sucked in a breath to reply and then swallowed it. Crotch Guy was a cop? He'd been trying to help us after all. He must have been working undercover. I flashed on how he'd tried to offer me gum in the laundry room. Was he an American? Did he know who we were? Had he called Warren? Blast. What if he *had* called Warren? I shuddered at the thought of the lecture I was going to get for impeding some sort of international investigation. I was pretty sure Mom would have an anecdote for that.

"...do you want to risk it?"

I realized that Morgan was still talking. And holding a

Rubik's Cube keychain under my nose. *Hey, those were Suit Guy's keys.*

A bronze-skinned lady in a hairnet grabbed Morgan's arm. "The tunnel."

Maybe she'd come in that way too.

She snatched the keys and screamed something in Spanish.

Without missing a beat, a bunch of ladies in matching rose colored dresses and starched white aprons dropped out of the crowd and changed direction.

Morgan and I backed into the stairwell. We were about to get run over.

18

The crowd of angry ladies dragged us down the flight of stairs and back to the laundry room that we'd escaped only a few hours before. A lone bulb swung in a far corner and flickered, casting long shadows off the washers and dryers. Water dripped into puddles here and there and the floor was littered with pipes and things that should have been tucked up in the ceiling. Like the rest of the lights. We made our way through the anxious crowd to the metal door where Hair Net Lady was fiddling with the keys in near darkness.

Morgan tossed his flashlight to one of her accomplices and I got to thinking about what might be waiting for us on the other side of that door. Definitely more bad guys. In the movies, the first person through always gets shot. I thought about that for about two seconds and casually slid to one side. Or tried to. Morgan caught my arm and pulled me back.

"Maybe I should hold the gun," he whispered. "I'm a better shot."

"I'm not that bad a shot." As long as the target wasn't moving. And was about five feet away. *Wait.* "Where did you get a gun?" I asked him. That would have come in handy back in that stupid alley.

Morgan squinted his eyes at me. "You have the gun, June."

"I don't...." *Uh oh.* I flashed on the shiny silver handgun that Suit Guy had stuck in his shoulder holster. It must have fallen on the floor when I'd dragged him out into the hall. Morgan had taken his keys and then probably figured I'd been smart enough to grab the gun. Blast. I wish I'd been smart enough to grab the gun.

"The only reason we're going this way is cause I thought you had...." Morgan held up a finger and leaned in close. "You know, the first one through the door usually...." We both took a couple of steps to one side.

Not that we were in any immediate danger. Hair Net Lady still wasn't having any luck with the keys and there weren't that many on the ring. Maybe she wouldn't get the door open. And if she did, maybe there wouldn't be anybody at the other end of the tunnel. Would they really have people sitting around guarding it day and night? And if they did, maybe we'd have surprise on our side. Suit Guy's goons probably weren't expecting to be overrun by a bunch of angry hotel workers. Still. I bent down and picked up a pipe. A lady next to me did the same and pretty soon, everyone was armed. Something about the expressions on the faces around me made me feel a little afraid for whoever was at the other end of that tunnel.

There was a cheer and Hair Net Lady flung the door opened. I tensed, half expecting bad guys to leap out, guns blazing.

"Ow."

Morgan pried my fingernails out of his arm.

"Sorry."

The ladies pushed around me for a spot up front as the flashlight lit up a closet that held a single vacuum cleaner.

Blast. I was sure that the tunnel had been behind that door.

Before anybody could freak out, Morgan stepped around me and pressed a palm against the wall behind the vacuum. It swung wide as oohs and ahhs spread through the crowd.

Beyond the closet, strings of Christmas lights twinkled along the ceiling of the dark tunnel, creating a multi-colored sky that stretched off to a far point in the distance. If circumstances had been different I would have thought it was beautiful.

Hair Net Lady held up a fist and shouted some words in Spanish. My stomach leaped into my throat as the words echoed. Fantastic way to let the bad guys know we were on our way.

There was a breath on my cheek and Morgan whispered in my ear, "For the oppressed, we take back our lives." He listened for a moment, "Neymar's gang aren't the only ones who use this tunnel. The ladies thought they were coming here to go to school but they were put to work in the hotel instead. We need to call Warren to help them."

"We can't even call Warren to help ourselves."

The women all began to chant and Hair Net Lady let out a battle cry that was echoed by the others. The ladies flowed into the tunnel, pipes help high and I pressed myself against the wall, afraid that I was going to be pulled along. Or run over. As the laundry emptied out, I could hear a dull roar in the distance. And some clanging sounds. And a lot of what sounded like manly screams. I took a couple of steps back and bumped into a washer. Whatever was happening, I knew I didn't want any part of it.

"Maybe we should just hop the fence after all," I said looking over at Morgan. Or at where he'd just been standing. "Morgan?" I ran into the tunnel fully expecting to see his mangled and twisted body stretched across the dirt floor. Instead, I found him crouched beside an overturned plastic tub.

"What is it?" I asked.

"Empty." He pointed his flashlight up the tunnel. There were more plastic tubs. Some overturned, some crushed. "Hang on."

He got up and I followed him to one that had somehow survived the carnage. He handed me the flashlight and knelt down beside it.

"What's in it?" I leaned in closer fully expecting to see some type of weapons. The tunnel was obviously being used to smuggle things into the US. Rifles? Machine guns? Rocket launchers? Drugs?

Morgan held up an oversized denim purse covered in rhinestones. I squinted at the word *Flaunt* stenciled on a metallic buckle on the front. The line crossing the t was angled from upper left to lower right. It should have been the other way around. Not that I was an accessory junkie. But I'd been known to wander the occasional flea market so I'd seen plenty of these knock-offs. And that made me laugh. Junior gangster Suit Guy was just a hood pushing counterfeit purses.

"Listen," Morgan said.

"To what?" Oh right. I didn't hear anything. Whatever had been going on, was over.

I dropped the purse back into the bin and followed Morgan up the tunnel.

Eventually, we climbed up a set of stone steps into what looked like somebody's kitchen. After someone else had stolen all their appliances. The house had to have been a foreclosure. Even the light fixtures had been ripped out. A table and four chairs were over-turned in the center of the room. Cards and poker chips spilled across the floor. There'd probably been cash too but the ladies would have taken care of that.

We slipped out the kitchen door into the side yard. There weren't any houses nearby. Or signs of the women. Or whomever had been at the poker table. On our left, a dirt path disappeared up a steep hill covered in a thick grove of mesquite trees. On the right, a empty driveway over-looked the most beautiful view of Nogales that I'd ever seen.

"Meaty Pete's," I yelled, pointing. The yellow and green roof of the fast food joint was unmistakable. Yeah. I was still hungry. A few streets over, I spotted another landmark. "A Filmore Lending!" It was a branch of my bank. Even without ID, I'd be able to get cash. They used one of those fingerprint scanner thingies. And the manager was a massive *Dewzer*. "We can get a taxi."

I looked around for Morgan and realized I was alone. Blast.

Where had he gone? I followed the driveway around to the front of the house. There he was. Sitting in a rusted out Volkswagen Convertible, fumbling around in the glove box. *The ladies had missed one.*

I may have bounced up and down a few times and clapped my hands.

We were going to get home. Dewey was going to be saved. I realized at that moment that I didn't want to take a leave of absence. I didn't want to try out archeology and all that dirty dirt. I just wanted to head straight to Dewey's house, soak in his hot tub and set up his next set of personal appearances. After we'd gotten him out of jail, of course.

"Never mind." Morgan got out of the car. "No keys."

"Are you sure?" I leaned in the driver's side, feeling around for the key slot and caught sight of the tall skinny stick shift. Blast. It was a manual. I loved driving those.

"We could always throw it in neutral and coast down the hill."

"Really?" I asked.

"Yeah," he said. "You get in and I'll give us a push."

I was so happy, I almost kissed him. And I would have but when I puckered up, he pulled back with a look of horror on his face.

"Oh relax…" was all I got out before he spun me to the ground and we rolled across the hot pavement. Chunks of asphalt exploded out of the spot where we'd just been. I lifted my head as a blood-covered rifle-wielding man staggered over the crest of the driveway, heading straight for us. He readied his rifle for another shot and Morgan dragged me to my feet and shoved me in the direction of the trail.

"Town is that way," I screamed pointing back at the rifleman. Rifle*men*. He'd been joined by three more heavily armed guys. Probably the poker players.

Boom. Boom. Boom. Trees around us exploded, raining leaves and bark down on our heads.

"Your way's fine." I chased Morgan up the hill and into the safety of the mesquite grove.

We were headed out to Whiplash Ridge after all. Maybe it would have been better if one of the bullets had gotten us. There was no way we were gonna survive the Ridge without water.

19

The rifle shots stopped after awhile, but we kept running till we couldn't. On the other side of the trees, the trail led us over a couple of hills that climbed steadily until we reached a deserted strip of road cut into the side of a mountain. I sprawled out on the hot pavement and threw a hand over my face to shield my eyes from the sun. I was in the middle of the road but I didn't care. The only cars out this far were going to be ones looking for me. Or herpers looking for snakes. And they'd be driving slow and slamming on the brakes, so I was in no danger of getting run over.

"Is there a gas station nearby?" I asked. I knew there wasn't. There was nothing out here on the Ridge. And I needed water. Now. If any of those bottles from the trash can back in Nogales had been in front of me at that very moment, I would have guzzled whatever precious drops of liquid they'd held without a second thought. Probable weird diseases and all. "Morgan?"

I could hear his shoes slapping along the pavement, moving farther away from me. Then coming back. Then tapping past.

"Morgan?" I lifted my head enough to squish my chin into my chest. I was all alone. Had he left me? I wanted to panic but I wasn't sure I had the energy.

And then I saw him, climbing back up the hill and onto the pavement, grinning that stupid lopsided grin of his, and holding...a jug of water.

I shielded my eyes for a better look. "Where did that come from?" Not that I cared.

"A lot of hikers pass through this spot."

By hikers, he meant illegals trying to sneak into the United States.

"Tree huggers leave the water," he added.

By tree huggers, I was pretty sure he meant himself. And probably Dewey. Not that I cared. I'd been away from Horseshoe Bend so long I couldn't remember which side of the argument I was supposed to be on.

Morgan dropped onto the pavement beside me and unscrewed the lid.

"You're dehydrated," he warned. "Don't drink too much or you'll puke."

"I know that," I said. I wasn't sure I did but it sounded like something Dewey would have told me at some point in the past.

I rolled onto my side and let out a pretty loud old man groan as I pushed myself into a sitting position. I wiggled my fingers at him and winced. I wish I'd grabbed more aspirin at Mom's.

"Ow." I made a fist and then stretched the fingers back out. "Ow. Ow. Ow."

"Stop hitting people," Morgan said passing me the jug.

"Soon as they stop trying to kill me."

I took a small sip of water. It was hot and stale and metallic and some of the best stuff I'd ever had in my life. I sighed and looked out over the valley below us. An army of saguaro were silhouetted against a sky that was melting into a deep purple, while strands of red and gold threaded their way across the horizon.

Morgan dropped onto the pavement beside me. "Beautiful, isn't it," his voice was almost a whisper.

"I guess." For me, the corner booth at Millsie's was more appealing.

"Can I ask you something?"

"Sure."

"Why are you wearing my clothes?"

He'd finally noticed. "Because mine are covered in your blood and Warren wanted to dress me in neon orange."

"Sorry about the mess."

"The blood or my office?"

"Both," he said.

"Thanks," I reached for the jug, "now let me ask *you* something. Warren said that there was like three liters of blood in your front room. And that it was your blood type. How are you even alive?" I took a sip and handed back the water.

"Do you remember Peggy Riggins?" Morgan took a small sip.

"No."

"She was one grade behind us."

"I don't." I kinda did but I wasn't interested in a trip down memory lane. I wiggled my good fingers for the jug and took a sip.

"She works at the blood bank."

And promptly spit it out all over Morgan. "I was covered in some disease-infested stranger's blood?"

He jumped up and backed away. I leaped to my feet and matched his retreat.

"No," he said, "they use this stuff for transfusions. If it wasn't safe, they wouldn't have it."

"And this Peggy person stole blood for you."

Morgan continued to back away, one eye on me, the other on the cluster of prickly pear cactus in his path. *Or was it cacti?* "She gave me stuff they were going to throw away."

I dropped the water jug. It landed on its side and began to roll down the hill, the precious liquid spilling out as it went. I should have cared but I didn't. Killing Morgan was suddenly more important. I took a swing at his stupid face, cursing myself when he ducked. *Always go low.* He skirted around me and then scrambled to grab the jug before it emptied itself.

"It's fine, June." But he still backed out of range as he capped what was left.

"It's fine?" I closed the distance and readied my fist. "Why were they throwing out the blood?"

"It was expired."

I finished the swing, going low, and caught him in the kidney. He doubled over, and dropped to his knees, one hand raised in surrender.

There was a rustling behind us and I turned in time to see a thin brown snake slither out of a shrub near Morgan.

"Time out," he yelled. He pushed himself to his feet and darted after the creepy crawlie grabbing, missing, and finally tossing his hands in the air in defeat.

"That was an Oxybelis aeneus and it was probably a male. I need a male. Jeez. It was right there."

"Dewey's locked in jail and you're snake hunting?" I kicked dirt in his direction.

"Oh get serious," Morgan yelled back.

"Warren will never charge Dewey with my murder. He loves the guy. Everybody loves the guy." It sounded like there were some issues there but I didn't have time to play shrink.

"You think that?" I screamed back. "Warren says that the DA will say that Dewey kicked you off the Costa Rica trip and when you argued about it, he killed you."

"But I'm not dead. Warren'll get the video. He'll let Dewey go."

"And what if he doesn't get it? What if the DA comes back from Green Valley early? First thing he's going to do when he finds out he's got a celebrity in his jail is to hold a press conference that'll end Dewey's career and it'll be all your fault."

"Warren'll get the video. And you'll be back in Horseshoe Bend before the sun sets. All you have to do is get back to the road, take a right and you'll run into a border patrol car before you know it."

A cushy seat on a helicopter flashed in my brain. "They're really close?" Wait. Did he just say *you*? "You're not going back?"

"I can't." He set the water jug on the ground and started down the hill.

"Morgan, we got away from those guys. Warren'll find your greyhound and he'll protect you both."

"Just follow the road to the right. You'll be fine."

"Why are you running away?" I yelled at his back. "You make me wanna scream."

So I did.

And it was loud. *Echo off the hills around us* kinda loud. I winced thinking about the bloody men with the shotguns. Had they followed us?

"June?" A voice drifted down from the road.

Hey, somebody was standing up there. We were saved. "Yes!" I waved an arm. "Don't leave." I scrambled up the hill, ready to hug everybody in the rescue party. Even if one of them was my mother. Turns out, it was just a nerdy, pale white guy about my age in a sweatshirt and shorts, standing beside an old dust-covered car.

"I can't believe I finally found you."

"Yeah…uhh…." I had no idea who he was.

He gave me an awkward wave and then tapped his chest. "Sammy."

"Right." It was the president of H.A.H. He'd gotten my email. And he'd joined the search party. If he'd been the one I'd puked on all those years ago, he didn't seem to be holding a grudge.

"Where's Warren?" I jogged a few steps in one direction and then the other trying to see past curves in the road.

"Oh, somewhere out here." He waved a hand over his shoulder. "You okay? You must be thirsty. I've got sodas."

A frosty pick-me-up sounded better. I knew for a fact that the

H.A.H. member kept a few cold ones on hand for emergencies. It was part of the reason I'd puked during my herping adventure all those years ago. "You got any beer?"

"I just might." Sammy grinned and headed around to the back of his car. I followed.

He popped the trunk and leaned in to fiddle with a styrofoam cooler. "Your note said Morgan was with you."

"He's somewhere down the hill," I said.

"Cool. Hey, can you grab that?" He jerked his thumb at a big-ass flashlight next to a tangled set of jumper cables. "The stupid trunk light burnt out."

"Sure," I reached for the light and was shoved from behind. I fell forward smashing my forehead into one of the cable clamps as my legs were scooped up and thrown at my neck. There was a loud clunk and I didn't need to look to know that I'd been locked in.

Two car trunks in less than twelve hours.

Blast.

I was the stupidest person alive.

20

"Sammy? Sammy let me out."

If this was payback for the puke, it felt pretty extreme. All the crap I'd gone through in the past two days ran through my head and I felt anger edge out panic. I took a deep breath and screamed, "Morgan!" Chances were better that this had something to do with that idiot. I shouted his name again and then held my breath hoping to hear...anything.

I didn't. If he was out there, he wasn't answering.

Or couldn't.

I'd have to get free on my own. I slid my hands around feeling for one of those I've-accidentally-been-locked-in latches. Blast. What were the odds that I'd be thrown in two car trunks in two days and neither would have one? I screamed and kicked the ceiling a few times but it didn't make me feel any better. I needed to concentrate and get out of here before...the engine kicked in and the car lurched forward.

Blast.

I fumbled around for the flashlight. It didn't work. The styrofoam cooler didn't have any beer in it either. Just a grape soda that I ended up spilling all over myself. *Sammy was such a jerk.*

I wiped sticky fingers on my sticky shirt and screamed at the ceiling in frustration. And then I kicked it a few more times. When my calves got tired from lifting my feet, I rolled onto my side and switched to where the taillights probably were. By the time I'd managed to knock one out, the sun was long gone and a partial moon wasn't offering much help. I stuck my arm through the hole but without traffic much less street lights, I was out of luck.

Before long, we turned onto a dirt road and the trunk began to fill up with dust. I wiggled my butt over the hole and waited for us to get to wherever we were headed.

This time though, I was going to be ready.

When we finally slowed to a stop, I played dead. The trunk squeaked open and hands gripped my waist. I thrust out my right arm, the jumper cable clamp clutched between my sticky fingers and thumb, and the sharp edge skidded across Sammy's scalp. He screamed and let go. I launched myself out of the trunk taking him to the ground. I got in a couple of punches before a voice squeaked, "It's me, it's me."

My arm froze mid-swing. "Morgan?"

Blast.

There was laughter and I twisted to look up at Sammy. He was leaning against the car watching us. The quarter moon overhead offered just enough light to tell me that we were in trouble. The gun that he had in his hand looked a bit like the one I should have taken from Suit Guy.

"You're such a loser, June."

He was right but I decided to ignore him for the moment. "Morgan, are you okay?"

As much as I'd wanted to hurt him over the past twenty-four hours, I was horrified that I'd finally done some damage. I pried his blood-covered hands loose and got a quick look at his scalp before fingers snapped back over the wound. I wasn't really sure why I'd wanted to see it. I had no idea what to do for someone who'd just been scalped. Besides collapse in a puddle of panic.

And then Mom's voice popped into my head. *In most cases,*

minor cuts to the head will stop bleeding after approximately fifteen minutes of applied pressure and have I told you about the woman who stuck a fork in her husband's knee and how their situation applies to you being at fault for everything that's happened this weekend?

I smacked the side of my head and her voice fell out.

"Give me your shirt, Morgan." I rolled it up his chest, *for a skinny guy he had quite a nice set of abs,* and past his face and then managed to pry his hands loose long enough to cover the wound with the wadded up fabric. "We need to keep pressure on it to stop the bleeding."

"How about we take this inside," Sammy suggested.

I let out a breath and sat back on my heels. I was getting really tired of people waving guns at me.

"What are *you* pissed about?"

He aimed at the dirt by my feet. The ground exploded into a million tiny fragments and I clamped my hands over my ears trying to drown out the thunderous roar from the gun.

"Shut up, June."

Or from my mouth. I bit my top lip and the scream went away.

Sammy pointed his gun at Morgan. "Help him up."

I let out a couple of quick breaths trying to shake the sound of my heartbeat out of my ears. "Give me a second here."

It took some effort to get Morgan up and moving. He was shuffling his feet but that was okay. Our steps needed to be small. And slow. I had to have time to come up with a plan. I gave the area a casual once-over searching for anything I could use to save us. There wasn't much. Just a lot of prickly pear cactus...cacti...*cactus?* Blast. I'd lived here most of my silly life. Why couldn't I ever remember which word was right?

"Keep moving."

I hadn't realized I'd stopped. "Sorry." I didn't mean it, of course.

I got Morgan shuffling again and I went back to my study of the neighborhood. Or lack there of. Not a single house in sight and the road that led here from the highway was probably his driveway. Nobody else would be coming this way unless they were visiting Sammy. On purpose. Since he was such a jerk, I doubted that happened very often.

We were going to die. Which was really inconvenient. Dewey was running out of time.

"Head to the back," Sammy said.

There were no outside lights and I stumbled over something that might have been a garden hose. Sammy caught me and I was tempted to slam an elbow into his ribs. But by the time the thought left my brain for my arm, he'd moved out of reach.

"There's a door right around the corner." He must have decided that Morgan was in no shape to run, and that I wasn't going to leave him, because he jogged around me and opened the door.

We shuffled into a narrow hall, lit by a single nightlight, past a tiny guest bathroom and then a washer and dryer half hidden under a pile of dirty laundry. I wrinkled my nose. There was a distinct smell. Doggy, but not quite dog-like.

"Stop," Sammy hissed. "And don't touch anything, you're disgusting."

Even in the dim light I could see that I was a patchwork of stains. Purple soda, red blood, brown dirt and black grease from the trunk of the car.

At least I wasn't a jerk.

"What now?" I asked.

Sammy stepped past me. He aimed the gun my way and used his free hand to open a door. The room it led to was pitch black.

"What's in there?"

"Stairs," he said.

"Go."

I peered into the darkness. "I don't want to fall. Turn on the light."

"How about I shoot you and you fall anyway."

Jerk.

I felt around for a railing and guided Morgan onto the first step. Behind us, the door shut and I heard a lock click.

"I need to sit." Morgan's voice sounded small and far away.

I lowered him onto the step and joined him.

"Can I do anything for you?" I asked.

"Can you reach my pocket?"

I narrowed my eyes, imagining where he was in the darkness so I could smack him.

I heard a soft sigh. "My flashlight is in the bottom left pocket."

Oh. I found it and shined the light on a spot near his head. "How are you feeling?"

"Better." He held up a blood covered palm and offered a weak smile. "This time the red stuff is all mine."

And I was probably covered in it. I shook the thought away with the happy memory of all those shots from the 27th Street Clinic and waved the light along the wall to the right of the door. There was a switch. I jumped up and flipped it. Nothing happened. Sammy had probably taken out the bulbs. He was such a jerk.

I dropped back onto the step and we sat in silence for a long moment.

And then I heard a weird nose. It kinda sounded like...sniffing.

"You smell like grape," Morgan finally said.

"I smell like a lot of things." I shined the flashlight at a spot on the wall near his face. "Why are we locked in Sammy's basement?" I was surprised at how calm my voice sounded.

He let out a raspy sigh. "You know the fifty grand that Neymar thinks I owe him?"

Neymar...*oh yeah, Suit Guy.* I nodded. "I heard something about it."

He ignored me and continued. "Well, I don't have that kind of money. And I couldn't get a hold of Dewey."

"And you wouldn't call Warren."

Morgan squished up his mouth.

"Sorry," I said. "Go on."

He let out another raspy breath and then continued in a slow even tone, "I was going to sell my snakes, you know, try and get enough cash to get out of town for a while, but Sammy needed a favor and it paid."

"What kind of favor?" I asked.

"He needed somebody to go down to Nogales and bring back a truck he'd bought. He offered me five hundred bucks."

Uh oh. Large sums of cash and border crossing never led to good things. I'd heard plenty of cautionary tales from Warren over the years. For some reason, he always seemed to think I was one step away from a life of crime. He should have been more worried about who I hung out with. Or rather, kinda hung out with. Because of my brother. Blast. Warren should've saved the lectures for Dewey.

"June?"

"Yeah. Uhh…so why couldn't Sammy drive the truck back himself?" I asked.

"He said he was busy with the snake show and the deal was too good to pass up."

"So what happened? Did you wreck it?"

"No."

"Then what happened?" I was starting to lose my patience. Who knew how long we had before Sammy came back and shot us. I hated the idea of having to haunt some medium to find out why I'd died.

There was another long raspy sigh and Morgan continued, "He was late to the pickup point. I got bored and looked in the suitcase I found behind the seat."

"What was in it?" I didn't want to ask the question but it was hanging in the air.

His eyes dropped to his feet and he seemed to forget that I was there. "I don't know if it got too hot in the car, or maybe they'd just been in there too long…."

"Who?"

"Howler Monkeys. They'd been drugged so they'd stay quiet..." his voice trailed off. "You don't want to know anymore."

He was right. I didn't.

"I made an anonymous call to Fish and Game and left the suitcase where they'd find it."

"How did Sammy take the news?" A dumb question considering where we were.

"I didn't stick around long enough to find out. I left the keys in the truck and walked home. A couple of hours later, he showed up at my place saying I owed him forty grand for the... cargo...and if I went to the cops, he'd tell them that I'd known what was in the truck all along. He said he'd be back in a couple of days with a schedule of pickups I needed to do to make us even. When I added in what Neymar wanted..." he was quiet for a minute. "Playing dead seemed like a good idea." Another sigh. "What I can't figure out is why he was out on the Ridge today."

I shrugged. No need to admit my role in any of that. "What *I* want to know is, if you've been trying to avoid Sammy, why were you at The Strand this morning? He's the president of H.A.H. You had to have known that he'd be at the snake show."

"Because I'm stupid."

I certainly wasn't going to argue with that.

"If I went to Warren about what Sammy was up to, he was going to find out about the Mexican gang and there was no way he was going to believe that I wasn't somehow involved with at least one of them. I mean, what *innocent* idiot finds themselves trapped between two sets of bad guys in one weekend?"

I raised my hand and Morgan gave me a weak smile.

"So that's why I was at The Strand," he said. "I thought that maybe if I found some hard evidence that Sammy was a smuggler...."

"Like an address book full of his buyers?" I eyed his sheepish grin. "Morgan, real life isn't like the movies."

"You're not kidding." He rubbed a hand over his bare chest and a tiny bit of the lopsided grin returned. "If it was we'd both be naked right about now."

I felt my cheeks flush. "Excuse me?"

"I *am* the hero in this little adventure. Isn't that what you called me while we were waiting in that line of geezers back at the border."

"I did say that." His life on the run *had* started because he'd been trying to protect his dog.

"The hero always gets the girl."

Not this one. "I thought you had a girlfriend?"

"Yeah, Julia." And then he shrugged. "But guys will sleep with pretty much any willing female."

And just like that I hated him again. "How about we get out of here instead."

"I'm open to either option," he said.

Since *I* wasn't, I reached back and wiggled the doorknob, just in case it had somehow unlocked itself. It hadn't.

"Come on." Maybe there was another way out. I got Morgan back on his feet and we took the stairs one at a time. When we reached the bottom, I eased him back down and I did a slow 360, waving the light around me as I turned.

The small basement had a low paneled ceiling and was stuffed with junk. Lots of it. Stacks of boxes. Discarded electronics. A bunch of mismatched dining room chairs. A bike with two flat tires. Three of Santa's reindeer flanked by a couple of creepy looking snowmen…and a blanket of stars visible through a narrow rectangular window high up on the far wall.

"Hey, you think I could fit through that?"

"We're so screwed," Morgan said.

"Hey…" I protested, I was sure *I* could fit. *Wait.* We're so screwed…no…*I'm so screwed.* Where had I heard that recently? I flashed on the image of a giant red bird biting down on a finger and I shined the light in Morgan's face. He squinted up at me.

"Did you lose a big red bird recently?" I asked.

"You found Fred?"

"Animal control did."

"She slipped out of my car at the Cactus Rose. I think that crazy maid scared her."

"You were running away yet you took a dog, a snake and talking bird *with* you?"

His mouth drooped into a frown. "I couldn't leave them."

I sighed. "No, you couldn't." *Wait.* "What about all the creepy crawlies at your house?" There'd been three rooms of cages stacked floor to ceiling.

"I figured Dewey could take care of them until...well, you know."

Oh, I knew. This had gone beyond just saving my brother. A house full of reptilian creatures meant a never-ending science lesson for me. I needed to un-dead Morgan. Now.

"How do you feel?" I asked. Not that it mattered.

"I think the bleeding stopped." He touched the wadded up shirt on his head. Most of the blood had dried and the garment looked like it was cemented in place. "I can't really feel anything."

"Great." I grabbed his arm and yanked him to his feet.

"Ow, what are you doing?"

"We're getting out of here." I used the flashlight to guide us through the mess to the window.

"I'm not going to fit through that," he said.

"It's not that small, I'll go first."

Morgan eyed the size of our escape route and then made a point of looking at my hips. "Okay."

I ignored the implication and balanced the flashlight in Rudolph's antlers so that it pointed in the general direction of the window. "Just crouch down."

It took some doing but I managed to climb onto his shoulders without actually touching the blood dried shirt on his head and he rose to his feet. The ceiling came at me fast and I scrunched down in time to avoid hitting my head. The motion unbalanced

Morgan and he staggered backwards. I leaned forward trying to keep us horizontal and it worked. Too well. Our new direction sent us straight for the wall. My forehead hitting the wall stopped us in our tracks.

I blinked a few times and watched the stars beyond the window begin to spin.

"June, let go."

"What?" I wasn't holding onto anything. Other than my head.

"My neck," Morgan sounded like he was being strangled. He slapped my leg a couple of times and I unclenched my thighs.

"Sorry," I said. I tapped his right shoulder. "Slide over a couple of steps."

He did and I gripped the edge of the window and tried to slide it open. It wouldn't budge.

"June," Morgan said.

"Yeah."

"Not that you're heavy but you are so could you hurry?"

"It. Won't. Open." My hands slipped off the frame and my bruised knuckles skidded across the glass. I punctuated my pain with a couple of my favorite words. "We're going to have to break it," I said.

"Is it locked?"

Blast. It was.

I lifted the latch to the up position and slid the window to the left. A gush of cold desert air invaded my lungs, and goose-bumps broke out over every bit of my exposed skin. My teeth chattered and I thought about the long sleeved gingham shirt that I'd left back in the hallway at The Strand Hotel.

"June," Morgan urged.

"I'm going." The gravel from the driveway extended all the way to the house and I reached out and flicked away as much of it as I could before I dug my elbows into mostly bare ground and pulled myself out the window. Or rather, halfway out. Somewhere around my hips, I got stuck.

Blast.

I wiggled my feet. "Help."

I felt hands on my ass. Hey, I did not want Morgan's hands there. "Don't…" was all I got out before he shoved me free and I skidded across the gravel on my stomach. I coughed away a cloud of dust and rocked myself into a sitting position. At least my t-shirt was one color now. Gravel gray. Something twinkled off the back of my hand and I held it up in the moonlight for a better look. A little white rock was imbedded in the skin. *Ow.* I carefully plucked it out and blew air on the dent it left behind. *Ow, ow, ow.* It still hurt so I rubbed my left palm over it and was dismayed to see all the stones stuck on the back of my wrist. And arm. Arms.

Blast.

I grit my teeth and ran my hands over pretty much all my exposed skin, knocking all the little white rocks free.

Ow, ow, ow, ow, ow.

When I was done, I realized that I was still sitting in Sammy's driveway all by myself.

"Morgan?" I made my way back over to the window and leaned in. "What are you doing?"

He didn't appear to be doing anything. He was sitting next to Rudolph with a weird look on his face.

"You ready?" I asked.

"I don't feel so good." Then he leaned over and puked on the red-nosed reindeer.

My stomach did a sympathetic roll. I sucked in a mouthful of cold air and looked away. When the puke noises stopped I looked back in the window, careful not to make eye contact with the reindeer.

"How about now?"

"Forget me," he said. "Get to the highway. It's east. Get help."

"East?" The sun was down. How was I supposed to know which direction was east?

A flash of silver buzzed by my head and there was a clanking noise in the gravel by my feet. I scooped up a little round case and popped it open. A needle floated inside a dial of glow-in-the-dark numbers. "You carry a compass?"

"Duh, June," he sighed. "I'm a herper."

"This doesn't really help," I said, "since I still can't see where I'm...."

Morgan's flashlight hit the gravel near my knee.

"...going." I picked it up and leaned back in the window.

"What are you doing?" he whispered. "Go east. Find help."

I glanced back at Sammy's driveway and thought about all the warm blooded creepy crawlies that wandered the desert at night. Coyotes. Bobcats. Javelinas. Guys like Sammy. Over at the house I saw a flicker of light in the corner of the front room. I crouched down and moved closer.

Through the picture glass window, I could see into a room up the hall. There was Sammy, his back to me, half buried in a bean bag chair, head phones over his ears, his body lit up by flickering lights. He was watching TV. And then he starting rocking from side to side. Or playing video games.

Or watching porn. It was Sammy.

Either way, he'd be distracted for a while.

I hurried back to the basement window and leaned in. "Morgan?"

"What are you still doing here?"

"Meet me at the top of the stairs. I'm getting you out of there."

"What?" He tried to stand up. "No, wait."

I didn't give him a chance to argue. I pointed the flashlight at the ground and hustled around the corner of the house, mindful of the garden hose, yet tripping on it anyway.

The back door was locked but the second window I came to wasn't latched completely. I tucked Morgan's flashlight into a pocket and after some wiggling, slid the window open with a soft squeak. I wrinkled my nose. There was that smell again.

Doggy but not quite dog-like. I whistled softly, prepared to get out of there at the first sign of an angry canine.

Nothing attacked so I heaved myself over the sill, rolled across a desk and landed on the tile floor with a soft thud. I held my breath. Had Sammy heard me? I dug Morgan's flashlight out of my pocket and played the light around the room. There wasn't much. A stack of cages similar to the ones back at Morgan's house, a couple of filing cabinets, a low table hidden under a sheet, and an over-sized ledger spread out on the desk that appeared to be full of names, addresses, and requests for rare and exotic animals.

Huh. It was a list of Sammy's buyers.

I ran a finger down the row of names. I didn't recognize anyone but that didn't mean anything. The book was thick and there were a lot of pages. Warren was going to be over the moon. He loved arresting people.

I set down the ledger and took a closer look at the room. A phone would have been great. Or a computer. Or an axe. In case Sammy discovered me. Of course, I didn't see any of those. I did spot a pair of snake tongs dangling from a hook behind the sheet-covered table. They were just like the ones I'd taken to the Cactus Rose Motel. Heavy duty with a triple coated rubber top jaw that made them ideal for handling combative species. Like that Maid. Or Sammy. In case I was discovered.

I couldn't reach the tongs outright so I tucked the flashlight back in a pocket, stood up on tippy toes and leaned against the table. My fingers wrapped around the prize as the sheet slipped, taking me with it. I came down hard, grazing my chin on the edge of the table, and sat back on my heels, dazed. As the sheet fluttered to the tiles around my feet I realized the table wasn't a table after all. It was a metal box.

An unearthly groan drifted out of the small air holes that dotted its side.

I felt the hair on the back of my neck stand up and I tightened my grip on the tongs. *Hey, I hadn't dropped them.*

"You woke her up."

I twisted to look back at Sammy.

He was standing in the open door with his face lost to the shadows, arms crossed, a stun gun dangling from one hand.

"You are the most annoying person ever." He stepped over to the cage, spun it to face me and raised the metal door. Moonlight danced over a whole lot of teeth. And then a dark shape leaped out.

21

A weird looking, medium-sized dog landed in front of me. Dark expressionless face topped by ears that rounded to points. Shaggy long hair that hung from its upper body. Wide shoulders that sloped to a butt hunched in an odd half-sit. Legs striped like a...zebra?

It took a wobbly step and choked out a pathetic *ah-ah-ah*.

"Goo-goo-good doggie," I whispered.

It wiggled its nose at me and a long thread of drool slid from one of its cheeks. Up close, I could see that its teeth had been filed down. And that it was pretty stoned.

"Eat her," Sammy yelled.

Blast. Wrong time to be covered in sugar and blood.

He waved his stun gun in the air and a fuzzy white line danced in the darkness.

Weird Dog's ears twitched and it leaped at me. I gasped and did that slo-motion kung fu thing, where I fell backward while a furry belly sailed over my face. My back hit the floor as I watched Weird Dog slide across the desk and drop out the open window.

"You idiot," Sammy shrieked.

I used the tongs to push myself to my feet. "What the hell was that?"

"Ten grand," Sammy yelled leaning out the window.

"For a dog?"

"It's a hyena. You can't even recognize a hyena?" He jammed a finger at my face. "You're an idiot."

I snapped the tongs at him. "Back off."

"You're such a waste," he hissed. "Right next to greatness and you don't even know what to do with it."

What was he talking about?

"Why does Dewey even put up with you?"

Oh yeah. I'd forgotten that he was a *Dewzer*.

I snapped the tongs again and he smirked.

"I bet you don't even know how to safely pickup a Crotalus scutulatus with those."

Blast. I hated it when the *Dewzers* called creepy crawlies by their scientific names.

"You're right," I said. "I have no idea how to safely lift anything off a curtain rod," I flashed on that article I'd left on my mother's coffee table, unread. "But I definitely know how to use these babies." I tossed the tongs in the air and caught them Louisville Slugger style.

Sammy's eyes widened as I lunged and swung low. I smacked him in the shin with enough force to bend the pole. He howled and collapsed. Somewhere out in the darkness, a unearthly howl returned.

I scrambled over his writhing body and shut the window. And locked it. And then dropped the blinds into place.

Finally feeling safe, I turned my attention to what was left of Sammy.

"Now, where the hell's your phone?"

22

S ammy was too busy wailing and clutching his bloody leg to answer so I stun gunned him. His body snapped into a fetal position and I had a horrifying thought. If he had his cell on him, I might have just turned it into a paperweight. I ran the flashlight over the pockets of his cargo shorts and then flipped him over with my foot, trying to avoid the blood but getting it all over my pants anyway. He appeared to be phone free and I decided to leave it at that. There was no way I was touching him.

I poked his shoulder with my shoe. "Where's your cell phone?" I asked.

He made a mewing noise and twitched.

Blast.

If it wasn't on him, it had to be close by. Nobody puts their cell phone down for long. I jogged down the hall to the TV room. There it was. Between the bean bag chair and a takeout box from The Leaning Tower of Pizza. I think I actually gasped.

LTP is a hole in the wall three streets up and one down from my office. The pies are misshaped, and over-sauced, and tastier than anything I've ever had in my life. The rumor goes that the owner, a freeze-dried little old lady, has been hiding out in

America since she killed a guy back in Italy in Nineteen seventy-two. It had seemed plausible enough to repeat often during my teen years. Why else would anybody move to Horseshoe Bend on purpose? Besides crazy brothers who like to wander the hills looking for creepy crawlies.

I stared down at the brick red box and my stomach gurgled. If I called LTP first, Warren could probably pick up a pie on his way.

I bent over to reach for the phone and grey splotches invaded my vision. For a moment, I felt like my head was going to float away and I threw a hand on the box to steady myself. It had been a lifetime since I'd had those Tacos in Mexico and if I didn't eat something soon, I was going to die. Die, die, die, and die again. Sammy was such a jerk. Leaving around empty boxes of the best pizza in the entire…things shifted under my hands and something inside rattled. Wait. *There were leftovers?* I shook my head to clear it and flipped up the lid.

Crusts. Sammy had left crusts. From LTP. Nobody eats LTP and leaves crusts. He was such a jerk. My stomach started on another chorus of *feed me* and I felt like slapping it.

"*Sammy cooties,*" I whispered. "You'll have your own pie soon enough."

I reached for the cell phone. My stomach took control of my reflexes and I picked up a piece of crust instead. And shoved it into my mouth. Garlic, tomato paste, and a hint of spicy sausage. *Heaven.* And then before I even knew what was happening, I was stuffing my mouth with things that had previously touched Sammy's lips. Stupid empty stomach. I flashed on all those shots from the 27th Street Clinic. Hopefully they covered saliva cooties too.

I was in the middle of chewing the dried cheese off the inside of the box, when I remembered that Morgan was still in the basement.

I grabbed a water from the fridge and let him out.

He drained most of the bottle while he looked over Sammy's

leg. The gash was still bleeding and after a quick check of the bathroom turned up nothing but a strip of those little round bandages, we couldn't agree on how to proceed.

Morgan wasn't all that worried. "It's not bleeding that much."

"I don't know," I said, eying the little red puddle that was starting to form under Sammy's leg. "I'd really like him to still be alive when he's arrested."

Morgan shrugged. "I guess we could put a tourniquet on it." He didn't sound like he was all that invested in the idea. "Too bad you're not wearing a bra."

"Excuse me?" What was he doing looking at my chest?

"Oh, calm down." He reached for the sheet that had covered the metal cage. "They make great tourniquets."

"I don't want to know how you know that." I dropped into the desk chair to watch Morgan try to tear a strip of fabric off the sheet. It wasn't cooperating.

"Any scissors in the desk?" he asked.

I jumped up to look. There was a pair in the top drawer. I passed them over and sat back down. He was about halfway through cutting off a strip when he suddenly stopped and looked up at me.

"You did call Warren, right?" He motioned to the cell phone in my hand.

Oh yeah. I'd gotten a little distracted with the pizza. And the blood.

"Is that phone wrapped in a napkin from LTP?" Morgan asked.

"It's preventing Sammy cooties."

"There wasn't a pizza to go with that napkin, was there?"

"Nope." Technically there wasn't.

"Maybe Warren can bring one with him."

My stomach let out a guilty gurgle. "I'll ask." I used the napkin to wipe off the iPhone screen and then hit the home button. A keypad came up. The phone was password protected.

Sammy was such a jerk. Since the guy was still out of it from being stun-gunned I did the only thing I could. I tapped the word *emergency* in the lower left corner of the screen.

The lady who answered wasn't all that impressed that I'd found someone named Morgan but she did agree to send an ambulance. Thankfully, Morgan knew where we were. Once I'd passed along all the needed info, the 911 operator agreed to transfer me to the Horseshoe Bend Sheriff's Station. Uncontrolled blathering helped. Moira answered on the fourth ring.

"Hi sweetie," she purred. "Look, it's really busy here, lots of bailouts. No news on you-know-whose-situation but we'll let you know."

And then she hung up.

Well. That certainly hadn't gone like I'd expected. It was almost as if she didn't know that I was missing.

I tapped the emergency button again. The same 911 operator answered and after some more weepy blathering I was connected to Mom's cell.

It went straight to voice mail. I held out the phone so that Morgan could hear.

"You suppose she knows it's me?"

He rolled his eyes. "You have a great mom."

I flashed on the strongest images I had of *his* mother. Vertical or horizontal, a bottle was never far from her hand. I supposed a conscious mother was better.

An automated voice informed me that I could leave a message after the beep.

"Hi Mom, it's me, your daughter June."

Morgan rolled his eyes again and I stuck my tongue out at him.

"Can you call Warren and tell him that I've got Morgan with me and we're at...."*Where were we again?* I held out the phone and Morgan leaned my way.

"Hi, Ms. Nash. Sorry about everything. We're at Sammy Renwald's place," he shouted, "712 Apache Plume Lane."

I put the phone back to my ear. "You should probably let Lucille know that Sammy has a hyena and it got out of his house." No need to explain my part in all that. "Oh, and there's an ambulance on the way cause Sammy got hurt." No need to explain that either. "And if you've got time, can you swing by LTP and grab a large with everything?"

Morgan held up his index and middle fingers.

"Make that two."

I left him with our former captor, neither looked they were up for a stroll, and went out to the front room to wait.

Warren's cruiser showed up first, him at the wheel, Mom in the passenger seat. They were followed closely by Lucille's animal control van and then finally the ambulance. Not the order I would have wanted to see if I'd been the one bleeding all over the floor but since Sammy had been such a jerk I was okay with it.

Warren got out of his patrol car, a gun in one hand, a bull-horn in the other. "Stay in the house, June, while we make sure the hyena isn't in the yard."

I cracked the door. "Did you get the pizza?"

"Stay. In. The. House."

"Fine." Mom had probably told him to skip it anyway. I closed the door and watched them through the peephole.

Over at the van, the side panel opened and a guy with a videocamera jumped out, dropped to his knees and then spun to face the open door for a cool shot of Lucille as she sprang out, long rifle in hand, followed by a guy in a familiar brown leather jacket.

"Dewey!"

I ripped open the front door and raced outside. My brother caught me mid-leap and spun us around.

"You're okay," I whispered. And he wasn't decked out in prison orange. In fact, he wasn't even dressed in the same clothes he'd been wearing when he'd been arrested. Or rather, deemed a *person of interest*. If Mom had made time to swing by

Dewey's house for a change of clothes, she'd definitely skipped my pizza. I should have said that it was for Morgan.

"I can't breathe," Dewey wheezed at me.

I loosened my grip. Just a bit.

"I hear *you* found Morgan," he said.

"It's a long story."

"You hate Morgan." He squished his lips against my cheek. "Thanks for breaking your ten-year streak."

"Only for you."

"June," Mom had taken over the bullhorn. "Stop distracting your brother."

I let go of Dewey's neck and he deposited me in the van. And caught sight of my bloody outfit.

"I'm okay," I said quickly. "It's not my blood."

He dug a flashlight similar to Morgan's from a pocket and waved it over my clothes. "What happened to you?"

"Let's just say, your best friend owes me a hell of a vacation."

"Where is Morgan?" Dewey glanced around the dark yard. "And does he look as bad as you?"

"He's inside. His head might need some stitches." No need to mention my part in that. "But otherwise, he's fine."

"Good," Dewey said, "on to more important things." And then he rubbed his hands together.

"How big is this hyena?"

I shrugged. "Labrador sized."

"Cool." He slung the strap of a rifle over his shoulder.

"You're not really going to shoot it are you?" I asked. It may have been a wild animal, but it was a victim too. Sammy was such a jerk.

"Mine's a tranquilizer. Lucille's here in case we need to resort to that. Hey," he bobbed his head at a spot just over my shoulder. "you've probably got enough."

I turned and cringed. The video camera was pointed at my face.

"Hi, June," the operator said, waving a hand at me. It was the same guy we'd had with us in Costa Rica. Eric. Or Paul. I'd only been half listening when he'd introduced himself and by the end of the first week, I'd felt silly asking. He must have lived close by.

"Hi," I said, flipping off the camera. There was no way I was sharing my pain with the *Dewzers*. Eric-or-Paul shrugged and aimed at something else. After three weeks of following me through the jungle he'd gotten pretty used to my angry finger.

The walkie-talkie on Dewey's hip crackled to life and spit out a bunch of garbly noise. He snatched it up and pressed it to his lips. The camera operator maneuvered around me to get the shot and I'm pretty sure Dewey paused long enough to make sure it was in focus. "Roger that. Our ETA is three minutes." He shouted Lucille's name and she came running over and pumped the barrel of her rifle. The camera operator made sure he got that shot too.

"H.A.H. thinks they've spotted our hyena," Dewey told Lucille. He turned and looked into the camera. "We'll have to be careful. A hyena bite can deliver eleven hundred pounds of pressure per square inch. I'm going to try to capture the animal alive and Lucille will be my backup," he paused for dramatic effect, "in case anything goes wrong." He flipped up the collar on his leather jacket and I rolled my eyes and imagined ten thousand *Dewzers* having a collective orgasm. He really knew how to play to his audience.

"Let's go find that hyena." He jerked a thumb over his shoulder, and he climbed into the passenger seat while Lucille disappeared into the back of the van. The camera operator ran around to the driver's side and the engine roared to life.

Dewey poked his head out the window. "You wanna come along?" he asked. I don't think he'd ever looked happier.

I shook my head. "I'll wait up for you." All I wanted to do was stand in a hot shower and eat pizza. At the same time, if possible.

We did an air kiss and the van sped off. I watched the taillights till they disappeared and then turned to Warren's patrol car. It was empty.

I found everybody inside. Sammy was cuffed to one of those rolling beds. He was still a bit loopy from me stun gunning him and the EMTs were having a hard time trying to figure out if he was allergic to anything. *He was such a jerk.*

Morgan was on the couch, somebody had thrown a blanket around his shoulders, and he was running down our little adventure for Warren while Mom cleaned up his head wound. He was at the part of the story where he'd decided he had to die so he could hide from Suit Guy and his goons.

I flashed on the gang back in Nogales. Had they made it out of the hotel? Had someone found Suit Guy in the hall? Had they put out the fire? What about Crotch Guy? Was he really a cop? And what about the creep named after a lizard that Suit Guy claimed he'd sold me to? What if he suddenly showed up?

"June?"

"What?" I was standing in front of mom.

"It's time to go."

"It is?"

The couch, where Morgan and Warren had just been sitting, was empty. And now the room was full of people. *When did they all get here?* I recognized a few of Warren's deputies, but the others were a mystery. A guy eased past me and I focused my eyes on the state police patch on his shoulder.

"June?"

"Yeah."

I let Mom lead me out into the yard. It was full of cop cars, Border Patrol, State Police and even a couple of news vans. I felt a moment of panic and Mom tightened her grip on my arm.

"It's okay," she said. "They're only interested in the animal smuggler."

Right. Sammy the jerk.

One of the deputies dropped us at Dewey's place, which made sense since I was living there, and mom helped me into the shower where I let the hot steamy water wash away the last two days of my life.

When I finally emerged, pruny and squeaky clean she put me in a pair of jammies and wrapped me in fluffy blue robe.

"Take this," she said. *Hey, there was a big white pill in the middle of her palm.* "It's just a little something to help you sleep."

I swallowed it without water, thanks to my only superpower and followed her into the kitchen where she had hot chocolate and homemade oatmeal waiting for me. Which was actually pretty nice of her. *Huh.* She must have been worried. Once she realized there was something she should have been worried about. I leaned into the steam rising off the bowl of oats and inhaled deeply. Raisins, chopped walnuts, apples and plenty of brown sugar. It was one of the few things I missed about my childhood and it almost made up for my forgotten pizza.

"You know, Morgan could have died because you wouldn't take the time to make one simple phone call."

And just like that it was ruined. "I was kidnapped too, Mom."

"You wouldn't have been if you'd made that phone call."

She was right of course, but there was no reason I had to sit here and take it. I picked up my bowl. "I think I'm going to lie down."

"And they have emergency services in Mexico," she continued as she followed me into the living room. "You could have called the police from any telephone in the country."

And then she went on to outline a dozen different ways she would have evaded the kidnappers and gotten Morgan home in time for dinner. I'd wanted to wait up for Dewey but in the end I had to pretend that the sleeping pill had kicked in, just to shut her up. And it worked. Too well. The sun was peeking through the curtains when I woke up in my own bed.

I snatched the fluffy blue robe off the floor and tiptoed down the hall to Dewey's room. It was empty. So was the kitchen. And every other room in the house.

I was relieved that Mom was gone but I'd kind of expected to find my brother. Or at least Morgan. He hadn't even said goodbye to me at Sammy's place. And after everything we'd been through together. Maybe he *was* still the same thoughtless jerk I remembered.

Or maybe he'd decided he was mad at me for almost scalping him. *That was not my fault. I'd thought he was that jerk Sammy.* I flashed on the jagged gouge I'd gotten a quick peek at before I'd rolled up his shirt and covered the wound. *He'd definitely been working out. Abs like that just didn't happen.* And why was he so mad at me anyway. I was the one who should have been mad at him. I'd been kidnapped twice, shot at, and sold to some underworld criminal named...after some kind of lizard. And all because of him.

Blast. I'd forgotten to tell Morgan that he owed me a vacation.

I wandered to the bathroom and shrieked at my reflection.

I had blood on my forehead. No. Wait. It was lipstick. Somebody had written on me. Probably Dewey. It was his style.

Fridge.

I grabbed a tissue and wandered back to the kitchen. Hey, there was a note on the refrigerator.

Missed you.

Yep. It was Dewey's handwriting.

Hyena's at the vet. Can't wait for you to see the footage. Sarah picked me up this morning.

I thought about his book agent's toothy grin and shivered.

Don't forget my lecture is at 3. When you need a ride to The Strand...

Oh yeah, my truck was still at the hotel.

...message Sarah. Her number's on my computer.

I crumpled the note. Not in a million hundred years.

An hour later, I was showered, dressed and squished into the backseat of Alvaro's car cringing as his granddaughter Ingrid and her *Dewzer* friends squealed over the stack of glossy 8x10's I'd traded for the ride.

"You think they'll want to shoot tomorrow?" Alvaro asked.

Along with a promise to tape part of an episode of Dewey's show *Gone Herpin'* at Millsies. Alvaro had hesitated when I'd asked for a ride, there'd been no one to cover for him at the bar, so I'd had to up the ante.

"Maybe," I said. Dewey's producer was never going to agree to shoot a nature show in a dive bar and I fully expected to be looking for a new hangout by the end of the week.

And it was all preferable to spending even a fraction of a second alone with Sarah Sunshine.

23

W hen we got to The Strand, the place was a zoo. The lot was packed and cars covered every inch of asphalt and grass within walking distance of the hotel. Alvaro maneuvered around a horde of *Dewzers* that stretched from a side door marked *Snake Show Entrance* and dropped us close to the front.

Ingrid and her friends ran over to the waiting crowd. One of the H.A.H. crew was saving them seats. Turns out she was a member. So I supposed it made sense when she'd asked me to pass her new email along to Dewey. I tried not to think about how much easier everything would have been if I'd have just sent that note to her instead of Sammy. I watched her bounce up to her friends and realized they were all staring at me.

Blast.

Had I been recognized? That really hadn't gone well lately and the last thing I needed was another entry on the *I Hate June Nash dot com* website.

I was pretty sure that Ingrid wouldn't have told anyone who I was, why risk anger association, and I wasn't wearing Morgan's famous outfit anymore. I'd wanted to put those jeans back on this morning but someone, probably Morgan, had stolen them. Since my suitcase was still sitting in an evidence box at the station, I was reduced to stuff from the back of my closet. I'd zipped myself into a pair of lady jeans, *the tiny pockets completely sucked* and topped those with a Gone Herpin' tee that featured a giant shot of my brother's smiling face with the words, *Good Adventures* splashed across the back.

One of Ingrid's friends patted her chest and gave me a thumbs up. Okay, cool. They just liked the shirt. I was safe. I nodded at the group, pulled my ball cap down over my eyes and slouched my way to the lobby.

A few people wandered in and out of the little room serving breakfast and a half dozen more lounged on the couches in the sitting area by the fireplace. Nobody recognized me. Nobody even looked up from their cell phones. Thank you technology.

I couldn't remember which room Sarah had been in, but I knew it was about three quarters of the way up one of the halls. Somewhere near the pool. Maybe. I figured I'd start in the corridor to the left and just work my way back here. If nothing else, I could knock on a few doors.

I bypassed the line at the reception desk and eyed the security guard blocking the path to the hall.

"I'm sorry, ma'm. We're only letting guests into this part of the hotel."

I moved closer to the guard and raised the brim of my cap. "I'm June Nash." I whispered. "My brother's Dewey Nash. He's the reason for all this today. So if you could let me through...."

A grin broke out over the guy's face. *Yes.* He recognized me.

"You're about the fiftieth person today to tell me they were Mr. Nash's sister."

People were impersonating me? What people? My stiff fingers tried to curl into a fist.

"Just call my brother's room, he'll tell you who I am."

He consulted his tablet and then shook his head. "There's no room registered to a Mr. Dewey Nash."

"Okay," I said. "It's probably under his book agent's name."

"Which is…?"

"Sarah."

"And her last name?"

Blast, I really needed to start paying attention to that kind of stuff. "Actually, the rooms would have been reserved by H.A.H."

"Who?"

This was getting me nowhere fast. I went over to the couch full of phone zombies and crouched down next to a girl with green hair.

"Do you have a minute?" I asked. She was so absorbed that I had to ask twice.

"Yeah, just a…." She glanced up mid tap. "*Ohhhhh.*"

That was more like it.

"What do you need?" She casually raised her phone for a selfie.

"To get to my room, I don't have my purse and this guy doesn't believe I'm me." And then I let out a sigh and rolled my eyes for emphasis. Like everyone in the world would know me. And considering who I was surrounded by, it was kinda true. "Would you mind showing him the website."

She bit at her bottom lip. "What website?"

I narrowed my eyes and she let out a nervous giggle. "O-kay." One more selfie and she nudged her friend, who nudged theirs and the three of them led me over to the security guard. After some tapping on phones and comparing different screens, they all gave me that same look that I'd gotten from Suit Guy and his goons.

"You kicked a fan in a wheelchair?" Security Guy asked.

I really didn't feel like going through that whole idiotic story again.

"Can I just get the room number?"

The guard fiddled with his tablet and then held it up next to my face. Out of the corner of my eye, I could see it was the picture of me on my mother's couch.

"Okay," he said. "You're you."

Unfortunately.

He tapped something on his tablet and held it up so only I could see it. *Room seventeen.*

"Thanks," I said. I took a step and turned back. Maybe if I was nicer to the *Dewzers*, they might return the favor. That stupid website needed some balance. "And thanks for your help too," I told the collective from the couch. I even smiled.

"Sure," they mumbled. But none of them were listening to me anymore. They were all huddled around the Security Guard's tablet. I had a feeling that *I Hate June Nash dot com* was about to get a new submission. And I bet nobody was going to mention how wonderful I'd been.

24

Aguy in a black t-shirt answered the door to room seventeen and I gasped when I realized it was Crotch Guy. A momentary look of panic spread over his face, probably the same look I had on mine, and then he got himself together and found his voice.

"Miss Nash."

"Hi…." *Guy I beat up in Nogales who I probably shouldn't refer to as Crotch Guy in person.* He hobbled to one side. Blast. He was wearing a walking cast on the foot I'd stomped. "I am really, really, sorry about…everything. I had no idea you were…." What *was* he again? Cop? Border Patrol? Mexican Police? US State Department? He didn't explain and I didn't press the issue.

"No need to apologize." The look on his face said there was a *huge* need to apologize. "Come in."

So you can kill me?

"We're almost finished with Mr. Durgan."

He shifted a bit more and I caught sight of the room behind him. Hey, it was the same one that Morgan had been searching the day all the craziness started. And there he was, at the little table in the kitchen. He'd showered and changed into a fresh pair of cargo shorts and a Gone Herpin' t-shirt that featured reptiles and their scientific names. A straw hat covered most of his wiry brown hair and the scalp that I'd accidentally tried to remove. Across from him, a trio in blue FBI windbreakers were scribbling away on yellow legal pads while he spoke. *Oh wait.* That was probably what Crotch Guy was. A Fed. He cleared his throat and they all paused to look over at us. Morgan grinned and waved and I wiggled a few fingers his way. He seemed pretty happy to be officially alive again.

"This is Miss Nash," Crotch Guy said. "She's here to make her statement."

"My what?" I didn't know anything about anything.

"Mr. Dugan has been instrumental in pushing our investigation into the Mingo crime family forward. Since you spent time alone with Neymar Durante Espina...."

"Who?"

One of the windbreakers held up the glossy mugshot of a smug guy with a hard part in his greasy black hair.

Oh. Suit Guy.

The last thing I wanted to do was relive the worst weekend of my life. Of course, what I wanted and what was probably going to happen were two different things. "I'm not talking to anyone," I said. "Not without a lawyer, anyway." And I'd ask for that friend of Mom's that nobody could find. That would buy me some time.

"I can sit you with, Miss Nash." A Korean guy in heavy black eyeliner poked his nose around one of the windbreakers. Blast. It was Harrison Kim. Apparently fresh from Metal Fest. I needed a distraction.

And then, for the second time in as many days, Sarah Sunshine came to my rescue.

"Junie!"

I turned toward the voice. She was across the room in an open doorway. No longer decked out in peach, Sarah was sporting jeans and the same *Dewzer* t-shirt as me. "We're twins," she declared and a thousand teeth sparkled my way. I shivered. And then got a great idea.

"I have to go," I told Crotch Guy

He drew in a breath and I cut him off. "It's Dewey's book agent," I said. "We've got to go over the logistics for today's talk." I pointed to Sarah as I started her way.

Her eyes widened and she nodded forcefully. "It *is* important. I promise to bring her back in just a bit."

"In just a bit," I echoed as I quickened my stride.

"But Miss Nash..." was all I heard before I was through the door and halfway across the connecting room. It was about a third larger than the other. A king-sized bed, a couple of sitting areas, a patio, a tiny kitchenette like the one I'd just left Morgan in, and a light crowd of people I didn't know. I stepped around a foursome taking selfies with a stack of books, probably Dewey's latest, and eyed an impressive breakfast spread laid out over two rolling carts. I thought about all the meals I'd missed over the last forty-eight hours, including breakfast this morning, and headed that way. I reached for a plate and realized that Sarah had followed me over.

"Thanks for playing along back there," I said.

"Actually, I did want to talk to you about today."

Some favorite words bounced around in my head and I stuffed a giant strawberry in my mouth to keep them from falling out.

Sarah tapped away on her tablet then turned it to show me a photo of the room where I'd run into Lucille after escaping from the three nanas at the snake show. The photo was a bit blurry but I could see somebody hovering in the door that led to the parking lot, the large cage by their feet filled with a big red bird.

"See, plenty of escape routes," Sarah announced with a smile.

"Yeah," I said grabbing another strawberry. I took a quick bite and juice dribbled into my palm.

"And did you see the curtain?" Sarah used her thumb and

index finger to widen the shot. Yep. There was a light blue curtain setup around the edges of the staging area.

"It will make a great backdrop for photos."

I shrugged. I didn't care about that. I just wanted to make sure we had a clear path to the door.

"And they're busy right now constructing a curtained walkway of safety from the hall up to the stage. Easy in and...."

"Easy out," I finished.

"Yes indeedy."

I turned my attention back to the food.

"Now, Morgan will be going down to the hall to warm up the audience at two o'clock."

And there was more. "Uh huh." I pretended to study the photo while I reached blindly for another strawberry.

"He's set to speak for 55 minutes, telling stories about Dewey, the usual stuff, meeting him for the first time as adorable little five-year-olds...."

I held up a finger.

"You won't be mentioned at all."

I nodded, peeled the little green topper off the fruit and popped the strawberry in my mouth.

"He'll finish off," she continued, "with a series of stories about snake hunting as teens, without mentioning you at all and then the fun starts. Max and Felix will be bringing in...."

Ooo. Blueberries. As Sarah droned on, I spooned a couple of big heaps onto my plate and then to keep them from rolling around I built a whipped cream wall. Cubes of melon were next, followed by wedges of pineapple, and more of those bright red strawberries. Then I came to the second table. Pastries, eggs, a variety of tasty-looking meat products, and no more room on my plate. Blast. I'd committed the buffet faux pas. I'd filled up with salad.

"Do you need some help?" Sarah was holding out a hand.

"Thanks." I gave her my plate and grabbed an empty one. She followed along as I loaded up on the good stuff.

"Then Matt and Felix will stay for...."

"Extra security?" I interrupted. You couldn't have enough of those guys. Especially around this many *Dewzers*.

Sarah tilted her head and squished her mouth up. "I suppose they can stay and help the regular security team."

"Fantastic." I folded a piece of smoky applewood bacon into my mouth. The crunching almost drowned out her cheerful voice.

"As I was saying," she continued, *Something...something... something...Dewey's name.*

"Where *is* my brother?" I asked. I'd expected to run into him by now.

"He and a woman with a very large red bird are being interviewed by the news." She leaned into a wide-eyed whisper. "Apparently, they broke up an international animal smuggling ring."

I had a feeling Sarah Sunshine had already figure out a way to turn the publicity into book sales. Which was actually a good thing. Blast. I had to remember that she did provide a useful service. "And they're doing this where?"

"Nearby," she said, "they started just a bit ago, so if you need him right now, he's indisposed. But your mom is out on the patio."

She was?

"Should I go get her?"

Dewey wouldn't be speaking for hours. Why would she be here this early? Mom wasn't the type to hang out. Besides, she hated creepy crawlies as much as I did. I looked over at the open slider and narrowed my eyes at the cluster gathered around the picnic table. No one I knew...no one I knew...no one I...hey, there was Leather Girl. She'd changed into a sky blue sundress and would have been unrecognizable if it weren't for the long blonde braid. I didn't see Mom in the crowd though. Wait. What was Sarah doing out there? She was still holding my plate of fruit and blinding someone with her smile.

I caught sight of flame red hair as a body forced its way from the crowd and pulled Sarah into a massive hug. And then Mom turned my way and motioned for me to join them. I shook my head like a catcher throwing off a pitcher's signal. I was pretty sure that she hadn't finished explaining last night why the world had nearly ended because I hadn't stopped to make a phone call.

I motioned to my plate and waved a hand around the room, like I was looking for a place to sit down. Mom's shoulders raised and lowered in a sigh and she pointed a finger at the picnic table behind her. I pantomimed pouring a drink in my mouth and then set off to find one, careful not to look back over my shoulder.

I skirted around the phone zombies who'd been taking selfies with Dewey's book and were now documenting the buffet. *Hey, there was a cooler under the fruit table.* I set my plate down and dug out a bottle of water. As I straightened up, I spotted Warren coming out of a bathroom. Before he could make eye contact and probably drag me back over to the FBI interrogation, I grabbed my food, slipped through a door and found myself out in the hall. Blobs of light exploded in my face and I screamed in fright.

"What the..." Locks of green hair came into focus before I was blinded by another round.

Blast. It was the *Dewzers* from the lobby, laying in wait for my brother. With flash cameras. *Who still used cameras?* And how did they get past the security guard? *Blasted Dewzers.* I threw up the hand with the water bottle, trying to shield my face and stumbled away from them, my eyes rapidly blinking as the dot obscuring my vision grew brighter. A cool metal bar hit the small of my back and I stood up on tippy toes and gave it a hard shove with my butt. There was a clunk, the door released and I fell out into the hot sunshine. I did a half spin, realized I was in the parking lot behind the building and turned back as the door clicked shut.

Blast. With my luck, the thing was probably locked. I set the water by my feet and gave the door handle a half-hearted wiggle.

Yep. I was locked out.

On the bright side, most of the good stuff hadn't spilled off my plate. I stuffed a little sausage in my mouth and my stomach grumbled a thank you. *Did I want to try to get back in?* There was a slim possibility that if I knocked, the *Dewzers* might open the door. Dewey *was* still in his interview though, so there'd be nothing to do but talk to mom. Or Miss Sunshine. Or Crotch Guy. I munched my way down to a layer of bacon and decided it would just be easier to head to the lobby. There was probably a bar. And a TV. Might as well be comfortable for a while. And hassle free.

I grabbed my water and took a right. About twenty paces away, near the end of the building, a small group blocked the sidewalk. There was something weird about the way they were all staring at a tall brunette. Was she someone famous? I squinted my eyes. *Wait.* Why was she holding her cell phone up against her forehead?

"Buccal pumping," a voice in the group called out.

"It's an ectotherm" another shouted.

"Komodo Dragon," the brunette squealed. "Latin name, Varanus Komodoensis." Another squeal and everybody started jumping up and down and hugging.

I almost spit out the tiny sausage I was chewing.

Dewzers.

I spun on my heels and headed the other way. In front of me, a long stretch of parked cars led to a familiar sight. The dumpsters where Evil Looking Guy had kidnapped me and Morgan. I did a quick scan of the shadows. Okay. It all looked good. Nothing out of the ordinary. No goon hovering nearby, ready to toss me into another car trunk. Still...I found myself tiptoeing as I passed the green bin...the blue one...and then the rusted old Volkswagen that sat behind them, idling and empty.

Wait. I knew that car...blast...*I knew that car.* It was the one from the tunnel house in Mexico. What was it doing here? I did a quick 360. No one in sight. And yet it was running, so somebody was coming back for it soon.

And then a shiny black nose popped up in the window. It bounced on the end of its muzzle and then squished up against the glass on the driver's side. "Rooooo."

Cyrano!

I ran over to the car, set my water on the roof and yanked on the door handle. Blast. It was locked. The shiny black nose squeaked against the glass and I realized she was trying to sniff the food on my plate.

"Unlock the door before they come back," I told her.

Yeah, she hadn't saved the day when Morgan and I were kidnapped, but this was completely different. I'd seen way too many Youtube videos of dogs opening front doors, screen doors, and even oven doors to not have a bit of hope.

Her eyes darted up to mine and then her long nose angled down toward the door lock. Had she understood me? Morgan *had* gone on and on in that Christmas letter about how smart she was.

"That's it," I said, "That's the lock. It's like a little lever. Use your teeth to pull it back."

She lifted her head and I felt a shiver run down my spine as I stared into her deep brown eyes. She knew what I was saying. She was going to save herself. She was going to…And then her long tongue uncurled from her mouth and started sliding all over the window in front of my plate.

Eew.

And she started bouncing, her butt knocking the stick shift around as she leaped from one seat to the other.

"Stop that," I told her. The hand brake had been pulled up but as ancient as the car was, I didn't think it would take much for it to disengage, and for the car to drive itself into the recycling bin.

"Hey, calm down." I tried hiding my plate behind my back but that just made her crazier.

"Rooooo...roooo...roo." Her frustration rose well above the noisy engine.

"Does it ever shut up?"

The hair on the back of my neck prickled and I squinted at the reflection in the car window.

Suit Guy.

Like nobody saw that one coming.

25

I did a slow turn and blinked at Suit Guy. He looked terrible. The bruises from the pipes had taken on a deep purple tint, his greasy hair had misplaced its part and his blue three piece suit was full of stains often associated with fires. And things that put out fires.

Giggles and squeals drifted down to us from the *Dewzers* at the other end of the building and I was motioned into the shadows of the dumpsters. I clutched my plate of meat and wondered what Suit Guy had in mind. If he shot me, somebody was going to hear it. Though, his gun arm didn't look all that steady. He could miss. Or maybe I could outrun him. Get back to the *Dewzers* playing that stupid phone game. Of course, if he shot one of them, instead of me, I'd never hear the end of it. I stayed put and kicked at the gravel under my feet.

"Surprised to see me?" he asked.

I really wasn't. He knew who I was. He knew who Dewey was. It wouldn't be that hard to figure out where we'd be today.

Suit Guy unhooked the only button still attached to his jacket and pulled out a crumpled add for the snake show. He shook it at me and seemed to be waiting for me to say something.

You can read probably wasn't it.

"So where's your friend?" he finally asked.

Surrounded by cops, Lucky Jerk. If I'd have just sat down and told the feds whatever it was that they'd wanted to hear, I'd be safe and sound too. And bored. And probably guilty of perjury because in the end I might have made something up just to get out of the room. Still. I'd be safe and sound.

"Hey." Suit Guy snapped his fingers. "Are you listening to me?"

What if I just sent him to room Seventeen? Crotch Guy could probably take care of himself. I'd been lucky and had gotten the drop on him in that alley. So to speak. And now he had those three feds to back him up. Of course, they wouldn't be expecting the subject of their manhunt to just show up at their door. They'd be totally unprepared. Heck, Crotch Guy hadn't even used the peep-hole when I'd knocked. And now Morgan was in that room. And Dewey was somewhere in the next. I couldn't risk them getting hurt.

"You see that smoke?" Suit Guy waved his gun at the field next to us.

I followed his line of sight and saw nothing but blue skies.

"That smokes's what's left of my hotel."

Since he was the one with the gun, I figured it was probably a good idea to humor him. "That's terrible. It was a beautiful hotel."

"She was my baby. You should have seen her when I bought her eight years ago." His eyes glazed over as he stared past me, lost in the memory. I took a tiny step to my right, to see if he'd notice.

He didn't.

"She was falling apart," he said. "Nothing like she was today. I brought her back up to the style she was accustomed to."

That got me two steps. I needed maybe ten more to reach the edge of the recycling bin. If I could get just a bit closer. I could get to cover.

"She was supposed to be added to the National Registry of Historic Buildings next month."

I raised my right foot, just an inch, ready to slide into my next step and Suit Guy snapped back to the present.

"What are you doing?"

I didn't know what to say so I stuffed a piece of bacon in my mouth.

"Did you just eat something?" He narrowed his eyes at me.

I shook my head and tried to move the bacon to one side of my mouth so I could answer. "No."

"I'm telling you about my hotel and you're having a snack and ignoring me?"

Crunch. Crunch. "No."

"Put it down."

"Okay." One more piece, *I couldn't help myself, I'm a nervous eater*, and I set the plate on the ground.

Over Suit Guy's shoulder, I could see Cyrano stomp her feet on the Volkswagen's dashboard and twist her muzzle until her eye was pressed up against the driver's window. What was she...wait...was she looking down at my food? Her jaw dropped open and a soft roo could be heard over the sputtering engine. That was probably a yes.

In my head, I could hear Morgan's voice: *Don't put stuff on the floor. That's her domain.* I gave the plate a little nudge with my foot and Cyrano began to whine. And wiggle. It started at her tail and by the time it worked its way up to her muzzle, the tiny Volkswagen was rocking.

"Shut up." Suit Guy spun and spit a bunch of angry Spanish at the little car. "Shut up." My plate caught his eye and he gave it a good kick. Bits of meat flew in every direction.

In the Volkswagen, Cyrano went ballistic, bouncing around and barking before dropping out of sight as the Beetle lunged at us. I threw myself to one side, rolling away, landing on my back, catching a view of Suit Guy as the car made contact, and then he was gone. The right side of the Volkswagen rose and fell and the car came to a screeching halt at the recycling bin, engine grinding, wheels spinning, gravel flying.

I scrambled to my feet. "Cyrano?" At the car, I pressed my face up against the glass and caught sight of the hound, safe in the backseat.

"What happened?"

I turned toward the voice.

It was the *Dewzers* who'd been playing the phone game. One of them stepped around to the front of the car. I flinched, prepared for the blood curdling screams that were inevitable. Instead, the girl tilted her head, considered the scene and then angled her cell phone and snapped a selfie.

Dewzers.

26

The next few hours were a whirlwind. Tolerated hugs from Mom, that new deputy Leather Girl, and some reporter trying to get a quote about Dewey, *who wasn't even there when it all went down.* Untolerated pat-downs from Sarah Sunshine and three different members of an EMT crew who'd all somehow gotten the idea that I'd been run over too. One of Warren's deputies managed to distract them by freeing Cyrano from the Volkswagen and after we were all treated to a tearful reunion between her and Morgan, I was parked at that kitchen table in room seventeen, where Crotch Guy and the three Feds asked me a zillion questions that I couldn't answer. At one point, someone came in and told us that Neymar Durante Espina, A.K.A. Suit Guy, was pretty banged up but he'd live to stand trial. A bit after that, a couple of pizzas were delivered. They weren't from Leaning Tower of Pizza, so I only had four slices.

I was starting to wonder what day it was when Warren showed up and announced that I was done. Crotch Guy didn't think I was but after a stare down, Warren won. I was handed a business card and told to call if I thought of anything else. I was pretty sure I wouldn't.

Out in the quiet, empty hall I fought an overwhelming urge to lie down.

"Your brother's talk starts in about five minutes."

"Yeah?" I should have been relieved that I hadn't missed it. Instead, I had to will myself to follow Warren up the hall, my feet dragging along the way, each step feeling like I was trudging through deep water. Or mud. I paused at the glass door that led to the Mesquite Room. Even out in the hall, I could hear Morgan's voice. And then a roar of laughter. And then Morgan again. The words weren't clear but I knew it was him.

"You don't look so good. Maybe I should drive you home."

My heart fluttered a little at the suggestion. My bed was waiting patiently for me. And if I couldn't sleep, at least I'd have the hot tub to myself. And I could order LTP on the Internet and I wouldn't have to share. On the other hand, I hadn't had time to actually look over Sarah Sunshine's escape route setup in person and I didn't like the idea of leaving Dewey on his own. Not after Philly and the bathroom debacle.

"Maybe I should take a quick peek inside." All I could see through the glass door was Sarah's blue curtained wall of safety. Who knew if it was really all that safe?

Warren leaned against the wall and crossed his arms. "Before we go in, let me ask you something."

Uh oh. He was using his cop voice.

"Do you know anything about the seventeen young women who showed up at the Guatemalan Consulate in Phoenix last night claiming to have been held captive in a slave labor ring in Nogales?"

And that explained why Hair Net Lady and her friends had been so angry. "I think we took the same tunnel back to America."

He didn't even raise an eyebrow. Morgan must have filled him in on all the sordid details.

"Do you think they might have set a fire at the hotel?"

But not all the details. I'd never told Morgan about what had happened in that room. "There was a fire?" I gave him my best *I'm innocent don't look at me* look.

"Yes. Do you know anything about it?"

I didn't want Hair Net Lady and her friends to get in trouble but I didn't want the trail to lead back to me and my bank account either. I pretended to think about it and then offered a non-committal shrug and grunt.

Warren gave me one small nod. "We can talk about it when you're feeling better."

Blast. I'd have to steer clear of him until he found something else to occupy his time. "You know, I was thinking, after the show, maybe you and me and Mom and Dewey can all go out for a family dinner?"

And that did it.

"I think I'll check on my deputies."

I waited till he was gone and then pushed open the glass door. A guy shaped like a bale of hay appeared out of nowhere and motioned for me to follow.

Mr. Bale O' Hay led me to a bend in the narrow corridor of safety where the space widened and revealed more guys shaped exactly like him, all arranged in a half circle. Sarah had certainly come through on her promise of body guards. And with the curtained walkway, it didn't look like there'd be a repeat of Philly. I was a happy camper. I'd say a quick hello to my brother and then go find someplace off to the side, to watch.

Mr. Bale O'Hay tapped two of his clones and they parted to reveal my brother, deep in his pre-lecture meditation ritual: head bent, eyes shut tight, fingers templed against his forehead. I was shooed in beside him and the half circle closed up again.

I didn't want to disturb Dewey so I tried to listen to Morgan's story. Something about a lizard. And a broken-down car. And cactus. Or had he said cacti? None of it made much sense and I was about to lose interest when I heard the words, *Whiplash Ridge*.

I slapped Dewey's shoulder and his eyes flew open.

"Is he talking about Sammy?" I asked. If he was, there was no way Morgan was finishing that story.

Dewey cocked his head to listen. "No. Where have you been?"

He'd been in his interview when Suit Guy had tried to kill me. Again. I guess no one had told him about it. "Pizza," I said.

His eyes widened. "LTP?"

I shook my head.

"So Morgan and I were talking. He feels really bad about everything that went down...."

"As he should."

He dug a business card out of a pocket. I took it and squinted down at the fancy gold letters.

Matfei Utkin Enterprises

Key West. Madrid. Odessa.

"I thought maybe you'd like to disappear for a while," Dewey said. "Matfei said you could stay at his house. He's never there."

"What's a Matfei Utkin?"

"He's one of the network's lawyers."

Huh. Key West. I'd heard about that place. It supposedly had more bars than people. I was intrigued.

"So? What do you think?"

I didn't get a chance to answer.

"Junie!"

I turned and squinted at Sarah Sunshine's teeth.

"I'm so glad you can join us!" she oozed

"Oh, I'm not...." And then I heard Morgan scream my brother's name and we were all moving. I tried to get out of the way but the Bales O' Hay were a wall, propelling us forward until I slammed my foot into the first step at the stage. Hand slipped under my armpits and I was carried to the top where Dewey, Sarah and I emerged from the cocoon of bodyguards and there was a deafening roar as a zillion *Dewzers* went wild. Blast. I was on stage. I never went on stage. I didn't want anybody looking at me. Especially *Dewzers*. Over at the podium, Morgan handed the mic to Dewey and I looked around for the quickest way off the platform.

To my left, the stage was backed with Sarah's blue safety curtain. *Why had I insisted on safety?* Behind me, the Bales O' Hay were blocking the stairs and to my right...*Dewzers*. Blast. Unless I wanted to draw any more attention to myself, and cross the stage behind Dewey to escape, I was trapped. I squinted out at the sea of cell phones all likely capturing video and tried to casually check to make sure that my shirt hadn't somehow risen up over my bra. That was the kind of luck I'd been having lately.

"Good Adventures, everybody," my brother shouted from the podium.

"Good Adventures," they screamed back in unison.

Morgan stepped around Dewey and joined me by the Bales O' Hay. "What are you doing up here?" he whispered.

"Not staying."

"How many of you," Dewey asked the audience, "saw the news this morning?" From the screams, it sounded like everybody had.

"Take a second to give some love to Lucille Gardner, Horseshoe Bend's own Animal Control Officer, who helped me bring that Hyena in safely."

Everybody stood, aimed their cell phones her way, and somehow clapped wildly at the same time. Across the room, a delighted Lucille waved back at them.

"Now," Dewey continued, "I have all the questions you guys have been leaving at the H.A.H. booth all weekend, so let's get right to it...."

I tugged on Morgan's shirt. "Get me out of here," I whispered. "Without making it look like you're getting me out of here."

"You should stay," he whispered back. "This is the perfect opportunity."

"For what?"

"For showing the *Dewzers* that you're more than a bunch of stupid anecdotes."

I felt a hot breath on my neck. "That is a fantastic idea."

I turned to squint at Sarah Sunshine's teeth.

"You should help with the demonstration later," she added.

"I wouldn't go that far," Morgan shook his head. "I just meant, be close, smile, laugh, look fun."

"No, it would be perfect," Sarah insisted. "It's all simple stuff. And she already said she loved it."

"I did?" I was pretty sure I hadn't.

"Back in the room, at the buffet."

Blast. I closed my eyes trying to remember what she'd been rattling on about while I'd been trying to fill up my lunch plate. *Morgan warming up the audience...stories about snake hunting...nobody mentioning my name....*

I shrugged. "Fine." Whatever it was, I could probably muddle through it.

Morgan leaned in close. "You really should learn to listen."

"What?" When did I not listen?

Over at the podium Dewey said something that made the *Dewzers* go wild again.

I felt a tug on my arm and I looked over at Morgan. His lips were moving but thanks to the crowd, it impossible to hear him. I tapped an ear and gave him my annoyed look. He grabbed my chin and twisted my face until I was looking at my brother. Hey, somebody was projecting photos on a screen behind him. They zipped through about a couple of dozen shots of different snakes before stopping on a photo of some long slim tools that made me think of the dentist. If you replaced the scraper at the end with a little silver ball anyway.

"Thanks," I heard Dewey call out. "That's the one."

Blast. Those weren't dental tools, of course. They were the things that Herpetologists used to sex snakes.

I tried to tune into what Dewey was saying to a lady in the first row.

"...we're going to go into a lot more details during the demonstration at the end, but you're right, there are other ways to determine the sex."

Which you'll show everybody at the end, right?

"But, since Edith asked."

Uh oh.

He lifted a long thick black snake. *Wait. When did he get a snake?*

"The first thing you want to do," he told the audience, "is locate the cloaca." He eased the snake around to expose its belly. "Look at the tail of the snake...."

"Hurry over there," Sarah whispered in my ear. And then she had a hand on my back and somehow my feet were moving.

"Use your thumb," Dewey was saying.

I dug in my heels stopping just shy of the podium.

"...To apply pressure...." I tried to look away as a tingly sensation raced down my throat, wobbled for a moment in my stomach and then slid down the back of my legs....

"...And Voila!"

Two pink antenna looking things squished up out of the snake and I think I squeaked.

"June?" The voice sounded so far away.

I tried to lift a foot to run, to get away from the horror, but I was weightless. *I was floating.* Wait. I was falling. As the stage rushed up to meet my face, I caught sight of a thousand delighted *Dewzers* lifting a thousand cell phones high over their heads.

Blast.

The End

Wait. That's not really the end. I mean, I didn't die or anything. I just fainted. And thanks to a whole lot of creative fans my worst nightmare came true and I ended up all over the Internet. I was photoshopped fainting on the moon, off the Eiffel tower, into a herd of stampeding buffalo and even out of a whale's blowhole. When the *Dewzers* moved onto a whole series of me falling on people: kids, cheerleaders, senior citizens toting oxygen tanks, and just about every flash mob that had ever been recorded, I stopped opening email attachments from Morgan and took Dewey up on his offer to disappear. An hour later, I was on a flight headed to Key West, the southernmost spot in the continental United States, ready for some peace and quiet. And a little rum.

I should have skipped the rum.

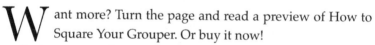

Want more? Turn the page and read a preview of How to Square Your Grouper. Or buy it now!

Did you enjoy the book? If you did, tell the world and write a review. Every time someone does, June smiles at a random *Dewzer*. That's almost as good as an angel getting her wings.

BONUS - CH 1: HOW TO SQUARE YOUR GROUPER

I was hung over.

And on a boat. That much I knew without opening my eyes. I could feel the deck sway below me, and a light breeze scented with salt and decaying fish guts was spritzing my face with drops of ocean. Somebody close by was fishing. I needed to sit up, so I could call them over and puke on them.

I peeled open an eye, lifted my sunglasses and squinted at the black blob that hung in the air just above my face. *Ew.* Nobody was fishing. A greyhound was breathing on me. The blob bounced on the end of its muzzle and a fat wet drop of nose juice slid off the tip, splashing on my cheek.

Blast. There was only one person I knew who ran with a greyhound.

"Morgan?" I croaked. My throat was scratchy and my tongue felt like it was wrapped in sticky layers of cotton.

"June! You're alive."

A pair of bright green swim fins slapped into view. I opened my other eye and lifted my head. There was Morgan, my brother's best friend and until recently my arch nemesis. He was wearing a black diving suit unzipped at the chest, *those abs still looked rock solid for such a skinny guy,* and holding a mask in one hand and a funny looking backpack in the other. His wiry brown hair was back to normal and sticking out in every possible direction. A few weeks ago, I'd nearly scalped him with a jumper cable clamp, resulting in a partially shaved head and a whole lot of stitches. In my defense, I'd been stuffed in the trunk of a car and had mistaken him for the crackpot who'd kidnapped me. In the end, he'd been a good sport about me trying to kill him.

"I'd about given up on you for the day," Morgan said.

Just past him, I could make out my reflection in the sailboat's white fiberglass hull. My curly black hair, normally controlled in a long ponytail was loose, and thanks to a healthy dose of sea air, had achieved frizzying heights I'd never dreamed possible.

I propped myself up on elbows, fought the urge to spill my guts, and realized I was wearing a teeny tiny bikini. I stared down in horror at all my exposed flesh. "Am I wearing sunscreen?"

"Of course," Morgan said.

I let out a little sigh of relief. Thanks to a chunk of Greek my misplaced father had grafted onto my family tree, I didn't burn as easily as my red-headed lily-white Mom. Still. I didn't want to end up with leather for skin in thirty years.

"I put it on you myself," Morgan added.

And the horror returned. I didn't want him touching my... *wait...*what was Morgan doing here? He was the reason I'd come to Key West. Thanks to a recent mishap, *that was all his fault,* I'd become a reluctant YouTube star and I was currently on vacation and not hiding out at all.

"What are you doing here?" I asked him.

He got a canister labeled CO2 from a nearby storage bin and began to hook it into the backpack. "You invited us."

That didn't sound like me.

"You called and said I should get my butt down here pronto. And to bring Cyrano."

The greyhound let out a whiny little roo and a drop of nose juice hit my shoulder.

"Then I heard you shout something about Zacapa," he continued, "and the line went dead."

That sounded like me.

When some people drink, they get silly. Some get mean. I get friendly. Not in the *I'll show you mine if you'll show me yours* kind of way. Though that has happened. But more in a *let's go shopping and do lunch* kinda way. For some reason, alcohol made me want to be friends with people I normally avoided. Like my mother. And apparently Morgan.

If I'd called *him*, I must have been drinking for at least a week. I had a vague notion of a cabbie taking me straight from the airport to a bar. And then nothing. Maybe I needed to lay off the Zacapa for awhile.

"What day is it?" I tried to lean out of the path of Cyrano's dripping nose.

"Friday."

Wow, I'd been drinking for a week and a day. Which explained my throbbing headache.

Then he grinned and added, "The 27th of April."

Blast. Make that one day. I'd arrived on the 26th. It really *was* time to lay off the Zacapa. I didn't want to wake up someday and find myself on a month long European river cruise with my mother.

"How did we get a sailboat?" I asked. "Did I buy it?"

Another sometimes side effect of my drinking.

"It's Matfei's."

"Who?" I know I'd never heard that name before.

"He's one of the lawyers with the show," Morgan said. "You're staying at his house. Though, it looks like you slept on the boat last night."

I flashed on a business card with fancy gold lettering. "Oh yeah." Matfei...something or other works for the production company that owns *Gone Herpin'*, my twin brother's TV show.

I'd needed to get out of town and he'd had an empty house. I tried to picture the address written on the back of the card. Which I hoped was still in my purse. And then I tried to picture my purse. Or rather its location. Lately, I'd had a problem keeping track of it.

"Are you staying at Matfei's too?" I asked.

Morgan's face lit up with a lopsided grin. "Would you like that?"

"No." I tried not to look at his abs. Life had been so much easier when he'd been my arch nemesis.

"I've got a room near Mallory Square."

"Oh." Wait. Something about this didn't feel right. I leaned on my left elbow and pushed the hound's nose away with the other. "I called you *yesterday*?"

"Before lunch."

"How'd you get here so fast?" We lived in the same sleepy little town in southern Arizona and a last minute flight had taken *me* thirteen hours and three connections on two different airlines to reach the island.

"The jet," Morgan said.

Yeah, that would do it.

Thanks to the popularity of Dewey's TV show, The Roar and Soar Network had given him unlimited use of a fancy jet. Of course, it hadn't been available when I'd needed to get out of town.

"Is Dewey with you?" I tried to look around the hound's nose, which was back in my face.

"Nah, he dropped me on the way."

"To where? He doesn't have anything scheduled." And I would know. I'm his assistant. I set up his appearances, answer his fan mail, and run interference from his weird hardcore fans, the *Dewzers*. Currently, Dewey's show was on a three month hiatus. And when my brother wasn't at work, he was out hunting the snakes and other creepy crawlies that he talked about *on* the show. There was nothing else in his life. I couldn't imagine where he might have been going.

Morgan shrugged. "He didn't say. I didn't ask."

I'd have to call Dewey when I got back to land.

"Are we done diving?" I asked. *I* felt done.

"We're having too much fun," Morgan said as he struggled into the oxygen-toting backpack.

"I'm having fun?" I was pretty sure I wasn't.

"You are. You've been watching Cyrano."

"Really?" I couldn't imagine how. It wasn't like I was in any shape to stop her if she decided to jump in after her daddy.

"I'm gonna get in a couple more dives before the sun goes down. Don't sail the boat away."

"Right," I said. I didn't think I could. Even if I'd wanted. I craned my neck to watch Morgan's green swim fins slap across the teak deck toward the back of the boat. There was a whirring noise, and a chunk of the railing began to lower itself toward the water. Huh. That was convenient. Kinda like the tail-gate on my pickup.

I let my neck drop back onto my pillowy hair and stared up past the folded sails to the poles and wires above. How many dives was *a couple more*? I lifted my sunglasses. And then let them drop right back into place. The fiery red ball was still pretty high in the sky. A couple more dives probably meant a couple more hours. Which was actually a good thing. I could get in a hangover reducing nap.

There was a splash and Cyrano let out a sad little greyhound roo and a couple of drops of nose juice dripped on my stomach. And then she poked me with her muzzle. So much for my recovery.

I drew up my knees, grabbed the underside of my thighs and ever-so-slowly rocked myself up into a sitting position. And got a better look at Morgan's greyhound.

Some sort of orange foam thing covered her back, clipped

under her chest and featured a convenient carrying handle on top.

I couldn't imagine why someone would want to carry a Greyhound around like a piece of luggage.

Then I noticed a rope dangling from the handle. My eyes followed it down her side, onto the deck and over to my foot where the other end was tied around my right ankle.

No wonder she'd stayed on the boat. Morgan was using me as a greyhound anchor.

Cyrano rooed a couple more times and I rubbed the soft brindle colored fur on her neck. "It's okay, sweetie. Your selfish jerk of a daddy will be right back."

She laid her long nose across my shoulder and purred. Not unlike a cat. Or a motorboat. *Wait.* I squinted past her at the ocean. It *was* a motorboat. Headed our way. Fast.

It zoomed around to Morgan's diving spot and I used Cyrano's handle to pull myself to my feet. And kept holding on as the waves hit, rocking us from side to side.

Down in the motorboat, three white guys who looked like they'd just stepped off the set of a hair-banging music video, clung to the edges of a black tarp that covered a massive bumpy shape in the center of the boat.

Two of the them leaped up onto the tailgate thingie that Morgan had dove from, one continued up onto the deck, while a third, still in the motorboat, ripped away the tarp and tossed up a lumpy bed pillow wrapped in plastic. The guy on the tailgate caught it and tossed it to the guy on the deck. He dropped it by my feet and turned to grab the next one.

Uh oh. Presents from random strangers were never good.

The guy still on the motorboat waved a hand at me. "You shouldn't let your dog sample the product. It could kill her."

I followed his line of sight to Cyrano. She had that first pillow between her front paws, and her teeth were well into the process of tearing away one of the corners of the plastic.

"Hey." I snatched it away from her and was smacked in the

face with an odor that could only be described as a family of skunks on holiday. I gagged and poked a finger in the hole.

This was not good. I'd been around enough stinky *Gone Herpin'* crew members to know what was in the pillow.

Blast.

Less than forty eight hours in Key West and I was a drug runner.

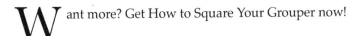

Want more? Get How to Square Your Grouper now!

ABOUT THE AUTHOR

Melissa Banczak has lived all over the country, thanks to her now-retired military spouse. She currently resides in Florida, where she's a reasonable driving distance to roller coasters in the Orlando area. An unexpected encounter with her daughter's nine foot boa, *Strawberry Margarita*, led to the idea for the first book in her June Nash *Mis*Adventure series. When she's not writing, she and her husband run. *Slowly.* She accidentally completed her first marathon in 2017, when she didn't hear her husband ask if she'd like to stop at 13.1. She would have.

She loves to chat. Contact her here:
melissabanczak.com
mel@melissabanczak.com

facebook.com/melissabanczakauthor
instagram.com/melissabanczak

ALSO BY MELISSA BANCZAK

Made in the USA
Columbia, SC
03 June 2020